My Deal with the Universe

"*My Deal with the Universe* is a tender story about learning to love what makes you different, featuring the coolest house I've ever read about. I desperately wanted to visit Jungleland and spend the summer exploring everything it has to offer with Daisy, Jack and Violet."
—Vikki VanSickle, author of *The Winnowing* and *Words that Start with B*

Feathered

* Finalist, Vine Award for Canadian Jewish Literature
* A CBC Books "Must-Read"
* A *Best Books for Kids & Teens* selection
* A *Resource Links* Best Book of 2016
* A TD Summer Reading Club selection

"Traces of Harper Lee's *To Kill a Mockingbird* and David Almond's *Skellig* run through the delicate narrative, which stands firmly on its own."
—*Booklist*

"Excellent . . . more than a regular coming-of-age story."
—*Resource Links*

"Engaging and moving in equal measures."
—*Canadian Children's Book News*

Under the Moon

* Finalist, Governor General's Literary Award
* A *Best Books for Kids & Teens* starred selection
* A *Resource Links* Best Book of 2012

"Highly Recommended."
—*CM: Canadian Review of Materials*

Girl on the Other Side

* Finalist, Canadian Library Association Young Adult Book Award

"Kerbel's depictions of each girl's very different brands of personal pain are stirring."
—*Publishers Weekly*

"Powerful. Anyone who has ever been bullied, bullied someone else, or thought that the bullying of others was wrong will be moved by Kerbel's story."
—*YA Book Shelf*

Deborah Kerbel

My Deal with the Universe

Scholastic Canada Ltd.
Toronto New York London Auckland Sydney
Mexico City New Delhi Hong Kong Buenos Aires

Scholastic Canada Ltd.
604 King Street West, Toronto, Ontario M5V 1E1, Canada

Scholastic Inc.
557 Broadway, New York, NY 10012, USA

Scholastic Australia Pty Limited
PO Box 579, Gosford, NSW 2250, Australia

Scholastic New Zealand Limited
Private Bag 94407, Botany, Manukau 2163, New Zealand

Scholastic Children's Books
Euston House, 24 Eversholt Street, London NW1 1DB, UK

www.scholastic.ca

Library and Archives Canada Cataloguing in Publication
Kerbel, Deborah, author
My deal with the universe / Deborah Kerbel.
Issued in print and electronic formats.
ISBN 978-1-4431-5756-8 (softcover).--ISBN 978-1-4431-5757-5 (ebook)
I. Title.
PS8621.E75.M9 2018 jC813'.6 C2017-906434-7
C2017-906435-5

Photos ©: Cover: Dreamstime: girl's body (Dannyphoto80); Shutterstock: girl's head (Samantha Cheah), dandelion (Valentina Razumova), dandelion doodles (NotionPic), (silvionka), (Valentina_Gurina). Interior chapter openers: Shutterstock: (Pressmaster).

6 5 4 3 2 1 Printed in Canada 139 18 19 20 21 22

For Jonah and Dahlia
Middle grade muses. Devoted campers.

Chapter 1

Let's just get this out of the way right off the top: My name's Daisy and, yeah, I'm *that* girl. The one who lives in the "Jungle." You know the house I'm talking about, right? The overgrown mess at the end of Bond Street? The one everyone stops and points at? The one neighbours complain about and mean kids throw rocks at? Well, that's my home. I live there with my parents, Nate and Frieda, and my brother, Jack, and our cat, Bobcat. You'd never know it, but underneath the tangled snarl of weeds and vines is a regular house.

In case you've somehow managed to miss it . . . well, if you're imagining the kind of pretty, quaint ivy-covered cottage you'd find in a fairy-tale book, I should stop you right now.

My house is not like that.

It's more like the plant version of Cousin Itt

from *The Addams Family.* That's a really old TV show, so go ahead and google it if you don't know what I'm talking about. But if you can imagine a giant, leafy, house-shaped, shaggy green blob then you're starting to get the picture. I'm pretty sure there's nothing like our house anywhere in the whole world.

Sometimes I'm sort of proud of that fact. Like those mornings when the birds nesting in the vines outside my bedroom wake me up with a chirpy serenade. Or in the fall when the leaves over my window change colour and it's like my room's been dipped in gold. But other times, like when the old couple next door yell at us and say our house is an "eyesore," I want to wear a paper bag over my head.

Mom says it's good to be unique but I'm not so sure she's right. Our neighbours hate us. Kids at school make fun of me because of where I live. They used to call me Jane (like from the Tarzan movie) and George (of the Jungle, of course). These days, they like to call me Weed — but with a really long *e* so it ends up sounding whiny, like a toddler on the verge of a really epic meltdown.

"Weeeee-eeeed!"

If you knew me, you'd know this nickname's all sorts of wrong because weeds grow quickly. And I don't grow much at all. Not since I was nine and the whole trouble with Jack. But I don't want to talk about that right now.

I guess now you're probably wondering what it feels like to live in the Jungle, right? My friend Willow asks me that question all the time. Problem is, I never know how to answer. When you've lived somewhere your whole life, it's not like there's anything you can compare it to. It just feels normal.

Except my normal isn't a normal anybody else would understand.

Chapter 2

"Can we turn on the light?"

Willow's yelling at me over the music. We're lying side by side on the attic floor and we're so close I can feel her breath on my face. The attic's actually my bedroom. I guess it would freak a lot of kids out, but I don't mind. The room's shaped like a mini pyramid, with walls sloping over my bed and my desk. On rainy nights when the wind blows hard, you can hear it swirling around, like it's going to lift the whole attic up and carry it away. Sometimes I fall asleep dreaming about where it could take me.

"Well, can we?" Willow asks again.

I shake my head. "Nope, not yet."

She pokes her elbow into my side — the ticklish part right under my ribs.

"Come on, this is lame," she yells, a little louder

this time. "It's four in the afternoon and I can hardly see a thing."

I don't answer because "Paperback Writer" is my new favourite Beatles song and we're almost at the best part and I'm trying to focus on the lyrics. This is supposed to be Junglecamp's Music History hour. What is she doing?

Suddenly, the music disappears. I open my eyes to see Willow holding up the pair of earbuds we'd been sharing just a moment ago. She's propped up on one elbow and she's wearing the same don't-mess-with-me-missy look on her face that Mom gives me when I ask for a raise in my allowance.

"I was listening to that!"

"But I'm trying to ask a question."

"I know," I say, reaching out to take the earbuds back.

"Really? 'Cause it doesn't look like you heard me."

"Of course I heard you. You were screaming in my face." I'm grabbing with both hands now. But she laughs an evil laugh and hides them behind her back.

"So, dude — can we turn on the light? I'm gonna fall asleep here!"

I sigh loudly and let my arms flop back to the floor,

gearing myself up for a battle. Willow's my BFF and I love her like a sister, but she's one of those people who rarely takes no for an answer. Plus, she always puts on this pitiful-cute face when she wants something, like a puppy begging for a bone. Teachers *always* cave. So do her parents. Last year, it's how she ended up with the first cellphone in the entire fifth grade. Sometimes I cave too. But not today.

I turn onto my side and put my face right up in hers so our noses are almost touching. She won't have any trouble seeing me now.

"You know the rules," I say in my best robot voice. "Not un-til af-ter din-ner."

She giggles, and robot-voices me back: "But how would your dad know an-y-way? We are up in the attic. And he is a-sleep down-stairs!"

That's not a joke. My dad's a security guard for a shopping mall. He works at night and sleeps during the day. He'll probably wake up in time to make dinner for me and Jack before heading back to work for his next shift, which starts about an hour after Mom's shift at the restaurant ends. Sometimes she makes it home to see him for a bit before he leaves. But if traffic is bad, they miss each other completely.

"I don't know *how* he'd know . . . he just would," I reply, ditching the robot voice so she knows I'm being serious. It's the truth anyway. Maybe it's because he's a security guard, but Dad's got bizarre radar for sneaky stuff like that. And I don't want to have to lie about it, just in case he asks. I'm the world's worst liar. Mom says I'd be pathetic at poker. That's the game where the best liar wins all the chips — except they're not actually potato chips, so who even cares?

There's an ant crawling up the inside of my arm. It's heading straight for my pit. I squirm as the tickle gets stronger, but resist the urge to flick it away. We have a be-kind-to-bugs rule in this house. Enjoy them, ignore them or catch and release them. No exceptions. That rule was Jack's idea, so we all go ahead with it. Nobody in our family argues with Jack.

Sitting up on her knees, Willow opens her eyes wide and clasps her hands together under her chin. Her smile glows brightly against the murky shadows of my bedroom. She looks like an angel in a Shawn Mendes T-shirt.

"Pleeeeeease turn on the light?" she puppy-begs. "I'll be your best friend."

"You already are," I reply, giggling as the ant reaches

my armpit. We've been BFFs since the day of my and Jack's eighth birthday. That was not long after he was diagnosed, and Mom and Dad decided to throw us a party to cheer us all up. They invited every kid in our class over for cake and cheesy party games. The whole thing was an epic fail. I can still hear the crying and screaming like it happened yesterday. Let's just say it was the last party my parents ever tried to throw here. All the kids were terrified of the Jungle. And the vines weren't even *that* bad back in those days. Most of the kids never made it up the front walk. A few of them got to the porch but turned and bolted before they could make it inside. Everyone except Willow. She smiled when she saw the vines. She squealed at the sight of all the little snails hiding under the leaves. And she actually happy-clapped when a baby squirrel poked its face out through the tangle of ivy covering the top of the entryway.

"Your house is fun," she said, breezing through the door, black braids flying behind her, grinning like she just won a free ticket to Disneyland.

Even though it was just the three of us, we played all the party games and shared the prizes. Willow told us to think of a perfect wish, then we stood side by side and blew out the candles on our birthday cake — Mom's homemade carrot cake with whipped cream icing. After Jack went to lie down, Willow and I sat at the table and ate the whole thing by ourselves. By the end of the afternoon, we were sick to our stomachs and promising to be best friends forever.

Even to this day, she's the only kid I know brave enough to come into our house. Willow's not afraid of anything. Gotta give her serious props for that.

"Okay, fine," she huffs, handing me back the earbuds. Her puppy face droops into a pout. I feel bad. With all the vines covering the windows, our house is pretty dark. Unless someone turns on a light, of course. But we're not exactly rich, plus Mom and Dad are big on energy conservation so they won't let us use electricity until after dinner. I know, it sounds medieval, right? Like if my brother and I were characters in a book, we would probably be living off crusts of bread and sleeping in a dungeon. But it's one of the few rules our parents give us, so Jack and I just deal with it.

Willow's family *is* rich, so she doesn't have to worry about things like that. I'm always offering to hang out at her house after school instead. But she never wants to. She says she prefers the "aura" of the Jungle. FYI, she totally learned that word from my mother. Frieda and Nate don't like labels, so technically they reject the term hippie — but that's what they are. Solstice-celebrating, incense-burning, barefoot-loving, tie-dye-wearing middle-aged tree huggers. They're all about communing with nature and saving the earth and living off the land and stuff.

"All right," I say, sitting up. "We can cut Music History short today. If you want."

Her eyes widen in surprise. I'll admit, I get a bit weird about staying on schedule. But that sad-puppy face is hard to resist. And it's only five minutes anyway.

"Great." Willow turns off her iPod and shoves it in her pocket before I can change my mind. "Boggle?" she asks, nodding at the collection of games I keep under my bed. Word games are my thing. I'm obsessed with crossword puzzles too. They sell big books of them at the corner store and I buy one every month with my allowance. I work on a puzzle every night to help me fall asleep. I'm probably the only twelve-year-old in the world with pencil marks on her pillow.

Shaking my head, I point to the white dry-erase

board hanging beside my bedroom door. Flicking the tiny ant out of my armpit, I scramble to my feet. There's just enough light to make out the next activity. If I squint.

"Not now," I say, tapping my finger on the four o'clock slot. *Nature and Environment.* "It's time to go outside and check on the raspberries."

Now I guess if you want to get technical, we don't really have to go outside to study nature. We could just go down to the basement where the scary things hang out. But the sun is shining today and we won't have to argue about turning on a light in the backyard. Willow nods and jumps up. It's only the beginning of June and she and I both know the raspberries won't be ready until July. But it's on the schedule, so we have to do it. No skipping out on activities! The two of us agreed to that when we signed up for Junglecamp. Willow's the head counsellor but I'm the director. The director's the boss. I made us sign contracts and everything.

It's funny, at school Willow's the one who's always in charge. But here in the Jungle, it's the exact opposite. I'm not exactly sure why. I'm not sure Willow does either. But we both like it that way.

I grab my puffer and we head down two flights of stairs, tiptoeing so we won't wake up Dad and holding hands tightly like they're superglued together. Outside, I blink as the daylight needles my eyes and I clutch my puffer hard.

"Just a quick check, okay?" I say. Pollen season's in full swing, and unless it's sitting on a pancake, maple is not my friend.

Bobcat's on his leash in the yard, curled up lazily under the chestnut tree. We need to keep him tied up whenever he's outside, to stop him from eating Jack's chickens. And also from attacking the neighbourhood dogs, who all think our house is a giant bush and go out of their way to use it as a community toilet. Truly. Every day, dozens of local dogs trek over to our house for their daily pee. It drives Bob crazy. If he weren't tied up, I'm sure he'd be off on a revenge spree. There wouldn't be a dog alive for blocks.

I keep a safe amount of space between us, just in case he's awake and feeling grumpy. Technically, Bob is my pet. My parents got him the year Jack and I turned nine. Jack got a pair of chickens and I got Bob. They called him a birthday present, but I knew better. The only reason they bought him was for pest control. They were freaked out after that one time I woke up screaming when a mouse scampered across my pillow. Jack says I must have dreamed it 'cause it's been years since he's seen a mouse in the house. But it's a true story. Cross my heart and hope to fly.

Fluffy and black with a long, sleek tail and dainty white paws, Bob had my heart from the second I saw him. But he's never, ever loved me back. He hisses every time I get close enough to pet him. Jack's the one he loves best.

Of course. Jack's the one everybody loves best.

The backyard is an obstacle course of overgrown weeds and stained patio chairs. Last week's laundry is still hanging on the line, waiting for someone to remember it. I make a mental note to bring it in later. If I don't do it, it'll probably stay out there till winter.

Standing on my tiptoes, I peer over the weeds and the vegetable patch and Jack's chicken coop into the perfectly manicured yard to the left. I breathe a sigh of relief. No Pitts in sight. Those two are so grouchy they make Bob look like a pussycat. In all the years we've lived beside them, I don't think I've seen either one of them crack a smile. And they definitely don't like kids — especially me and Jack. Pets, noise and vines also seem to be on their hit list. Dad says there must be a good reason for all their grumpiness. Just wish I knew what it was.

Turning back to face my own yard, I hold my breath and squint my eyes. And just like that, the weeds and clutter and smelly compost heap are gone. In their place is a campground. Lots of open space and rolling green hills. There's even a little lake in the distance. With a rainbow and a couple of fluffy white clouds.

It's perfect.

I take Willow's hand and pull her over to the raspberry bushes.

"After Nature and Environment, we have half an hour of free time before camp ends. So if you want to go back and do Arts and Crafts, that would be okay. Or we could play Bananagrams."

Willow shrugs. "Maybe both."

And that's how great a friend she is 'cause she doesn't even like playing word games. But she goes along with it for me. And I know it's not because I'm the director and she's just head counsellor. It's because she's the nicest person I know. And also the bravest.

But I already told you that.

I wish I could be more like her.

Chapter 3

Hurricane Frieda is blowing through our kitchen. Cupboard doors are hanging open, newspapers are on the floor, chairs are turned upside down and she's tearing around searching for her keys.

She's lost them. Again.

Mom's always losing stuff. She says it's not her fault she was born scatterbrained. I'm guessing the fact that it's so dark in our house probably doesn't help either.

"They've gotta be somewhere," she moans, opening the oven and poking her head inside. I sigh, leaning down to examine the plate of cheese, crackers and guacamole she put in front of me. On weekdays, breakfast in the Jungle can be a surprise. Dad's not usually around to eat with us and Mom's always in a rush to get ready for work. But every now and then she'll find some time to make me a meal. I think it helps her with the busy-working-parent-guilt thing, so I try not to complain. Problem is, with Mom you never know what you're going to get — except it's going to be healthy. She and Jack are the same that way. Dad and I are the junk-food lovers in the family. Mom doesn't approve, so we try not to eat the good stuff in front of her.

"I'm not sure this counts as breakfast food," I say softly, wishing I could just have a normal breakfast like other kids. Now I'm thinking about the box of Lucky Charms Dad secretly bought last weekend and wondering how I can pour myself a bowl without Mom seeing.

"Why not? It's a healthy serving of dairy, grains and fruit." Her voice is muffled because now she's rummaging through the fridge for those keys. "Absolutely no different from cereal and milk with a side of orange juice."

Actually, it's another-planet different from cereal and milk with a side of orange juice. I want to tell her that without hurting her feelings but the *clink-clank* of bottles and jars is too loud. A moment later she spins around to face me.

"Ha! Found them!" she says, holding up her key chain. "Right next to the pickles. Yes!"

She looks so happy I don't even ask how they got there in the first place. "Congrats," I say instead, picking up a piece of cheese and giving it a sniff. My stomach does a wobbly somersault. The cheese smells exactly like my brother's sweaty socks. (Unfortunately, I happen to know this for a fact because I'm the one who always ends up doing the laundry around here.) I toss it back on the plate and stand up. "I'm not too hungry this morning. I'll eat at school."

Mom's smile fades. "Are you sure? Did you at least take your vitamins?"

"Yeah. And I'll bring a muffin with me to go."

"Okay. And take one for your brother too." Mom leans over to kiss my cheek. "Gotta run. I can't be late again or they'll have my head."

I take her hand to hold her still for a second, and inhale the sweet coconut smell of her homemade face cream. She's wearing a red bandana over her brown hair, to cover up the grey roots she's too busy to dye. Up close, I can see the lines in her forehead that never used to be there. I reach up to smooth them out. She smiles and the lines soften. But only for a second. They come back when she notices my nail polish.

"Nice nails. But why black, Rabbit?"

That's my mom's baby nickname for me. It has everything to do with me being small and timid. And despite what you might be thinking, definitely nothing to do with the size of my ears. At least, that's what she tells me.

"Willow gave me a manicure. It's just a colour, Frieda. Not an emo thing. And it's not black — it's eggplant."

She lifts my hand to her face and takes a closer look at my nails, squinting hard in the dim light of the kitchen.

"So it is," she says, giving my fingers a light kiss. The lines soften again. "Do I need to drop you and Jack at school?"

"No, we can walk."

I don't want to say how socially damaging it would be to pull up in front of the school on the back of her polka-dot scooter.

She gives my hand a squeeze. "Okay. See you tonight."

Clutching her keys, she sweeps her purse off the table and dashes out the door. Coconut-scented air swirls in her wake.

Hurricane Frieda has left the building.

Taking my dishes to the sink, I grab two leftover muffins from the bread basket and cram them into the pocket of my hoodie.

"Jack?" I holler up the stairs. "I don't want to be late again."

"Coming!"

Jack's my twin brother. I'm technically older by eight minutes, although you'd never know it by looking at the two of us 'cause he's a full head taller than me now. Because I'm older, I get to boss him around, which makes me happy. His full name is actually Jack-Kerouac, after my parents' favourite author. But sometimes I call him Toe. Long story. Sometimes he calls me Laze — that's short-form for Lazy Daisy. Because there was once a cartoon character with that name who would fall asleep at the dumbest moments. Like on the toilet. Or watching fireworks. Or eating french fries. He thought it was hilarious, so he started calling me that, and I let him because it's impossible to say no to Jack.

Swinging his backpack over his shoulder, he appears at the top of the stairway, brown eyes squinting and shaggy hair ruffled from sleep. It bounces on his shoulders as he gallops down the steps. After it started growing back, he swore he was never going to cut it again. And he hasn't (except that one time he had to get an emergency trim last August after it got caught in a swimming pool drain when we were diving for quarters at Willow's house). Even though he's running late for the fifth day in a row, I can't help smiling at the sight of him. You'd smile too, because Jack is sunshine ice cream served up with rainbow sprinkles and chocolate sauce.

"Let's go," he says, bobbing up and down on his toes. He's like a giant puppy ready for his morning walk. Together, we head out the front door and turn in the direction of school, our feet moving in perfect time. It rained last night so the fresh morning air feels clean. With each breath, I can feel the maple pollen rinsing out of my soupy lungs.

"Why can't you come to breakfast once in a while?" I ask, play-punching him in the arm. He rubs his shoulder, pretending to be hurt.

"You know I don't do breakfast anymore."

"Oh yeah . . . artificially flavoured chunks, right?"

His smile melts and a pair of paper-thin lines slice through the smooth surface of his forehead.

Just like Mom.

It's always been that way. Jack got all her genes. From her hippy-dippy personality to her gap-toothed smile. The only thing I got from Mom is her weird toes.

"Don't make fun," he says.

I wouldn't. Ever. Believe me, living in the Jungle isn't exactly a ticket to popularity for either of us, so I know how it feels to get teased. But luckily, except for the occasional Tarzan zing, most kids at school leave Jack alone. Like I said, everyone in the world loves my brother.

I reach into my pocket and pull out one of the left-over muffins.

"Here — in case you get hungry later. It's oatmeal. And it's homemade, so you don't have to worry about chemicals or supporting non-local . . ."

The muffin disappears into Jack's mouth before I can finish my sentence.

"Dude. Slow down. You'll make yourself sick."

"Too late," he snorts, holding up his MedicAlert bracelet.

"Funny."

"Thanks. Make sure you put that on my grave-stone."

He crosses his eyes and sticks out his tongue like he's dying. Which, I guess if you want to get technical, he sort of could be. And then his face breaks back into a toothy grin and I can't help smiling too. My brother might be the only twelve-year-old in the world who likes to joke about his own funeral. I don't mind so much 'cause I know he's just trying to be funny. But our parents get super mad when he talks like that. Jack really can't help himself. He's always had an extreme personality. When he was little, he was so obsessed with dinosaurs, he spouted names, habitats and fossil records to anyone who would listen. And when he was learning how to ride a two-wheeler, he had to practise it every day — even in the winter when the sidewalks were all ice and snow, which is how he broke his leg on our fifth birthday. Then his first grade teacher did a unit on climate change. Jack hasn't been the same since. We were already pretty green, but within a few weeks, he had our whole family recycling and reusing *everything* — even our Ziploc bags. I swear, if Jack could figure out a way to recycle his own toilet paper, I think he would.

These days, Jack's extreme about food. He was always a healthy eater, but after his diagnosis he decided to go all out. Now he only eats organic food that comes from local, vegetarian-friendly farms. For our birthday last year, all he wanted was an industrial-strength blender so he could make top-quality smoothies. And then a few months ago, he started skipping breakfast on school days.

"The extra few minutes of sleep are more important to my overall well-being than a few bites of mass-manufactured, chemically preserved, artificially flavoured chunks of overly refined grains floating in genetically modified bovine juice anyway," he announced one morning. (I bet he read that in a book somewhere, but he swears up and down that he didn't.)

Mom and Dad call Jack an "old soul." I think that's probably true. He also loves big words, just like I do.

We stop walking for a quick minute to help Mr. Lee haul in his recycling bin.

"Thank you, thank you," he mumbles, grinning toothlessly as he leans on his silver-handled cane. Poor Mr. Lee. He's old and bald and lives alone in that big, empty house because all his family's either died or moved away. I think he must be at least ninety years old. Jack thinks he's older than a hundred but neither of us has the guts to ask.

When we get to the main intersection in front of our school, I reach to take Jack's hand. "Really, Laze?" he whispers, pulling it away. He looks around to see if any other kids are watching.

"Sorry, Toe," I say, dropping my arm. Last month he didn't mind holding my hand. How did he manage to outgrow it so fast? We cross to the other side in awkward silence. Truth is, I've always loved acting like the big sister and taking care of Jack. He used to love it too. When he was little, he wouldn't let anybody but me put a Band-Aid on his cuts and scrapes. And when he was really sick a few years back, he'd beg me to sleep overnight at the hospital 'cause he was scared of waking up alone. Every now and then I'd be allowed, as long as I slept in a separate bed. On those nights, we'd stay up late drawing buckteeth and kissy lips and giant moustaches on our face masks. And I'd turn off the lights and yell "Boo" and scare the nurses when they came in to take Jack's temperature. And I'd make up silly stories and jokes to keep him smiling, even when the medicine was making him pukey.

Wiping the crumbs carefully from his bottom lip, he folds the empty muffin paper into a nice, neat square and slides it into the pocket of his shorts.

I know he's saving it for recycling later. I bump his backpack with mine.

"Hey, Nate bought a box of Lucky Charms last week. Want to have some after school? You know you wanna."

He bumps me back. "You and Dad shouldn't eat that stuff. It's why you're so short, you know. If you ate healthy you'd be tall like me."

That's not true, but I don't come out and say it because I don't want him to know. Just between you and me, the real reason I'm so short is because of that deal I made with the universe. Plain and simple. I haven't grown a smidge in three years. Mom's taken me to her naturopath so often, he's tired of seeing me. I know this because the last time we went, he rolled his eyes and said, "You again?"

Seriously? What kind of doctor says a thing like that?

He put me on vitamins and told my mother to stop worrying. "She'll grow when she's ready. Just make sure she gets lots of fresh air and sunshine."

It made me feel like a houseplant. I was half-expecting him to point at me and say: "Weeee-eeeed!" He didn't, of course. But to this day I'm still not sure if he was teasing about the Jungle.

Yeah, I think he must have been.

Chapter 4

I guess Jack and I fight as much as any other brother and sister. We argue about all the regular stuff — you know, like who's the bigger bathroom hog, whose turn it is to do the dishes, who gets first dibs on the Sunday comics. But one thing we agree about is weekends. They're the best because Mom and Dad don't go to work and our family actually gets to spend time together. And that's so great, I don't even mind having to sit through a two-hour *Brady Bunch* marathon. (That's another really old show, in case you don't know.) Our TV is a big, clunky thing that Mom and Dad rescued from a neighbour's curb. My parents are obsessed with recycling other people's junk. Flea markets and yard sales are their favourite places to hang out. And every garbage night since I can remember, they roam the neighbourhood in search of treasure. The TV with a built-in DVD player was their biggest find yet.

They were so adorkably proud of themselves after they lugged it home and hooked it up. We don't have cable or Netflix, but they like to borrow old-school videos and DVDs from the library. Some of them aren't too bad. I like *Happy Days* and *Mork & Mindy*. But a lot of those old shows are so lame, I don't know how the actors managed to say their lines without laughing.

After the fifth episode in tonight's marathon — the one where the Brady kids go full-out Hannah Montana and morph into a singing group — Mom snaps off the TV.

"It's getting late," she yodels through a yawn. "Anyone else ready for bed?"

"No!" Jack and I say in perfect jinx time. It's only eight-thirty, but Mom's eyes are drooping like she's going to conk out any second. She tries to take the empty popcorn bowl away from Jack, but he won't give it up. He likes crunching on the half-popped kernels at the bottom. I scoot down the couch to the empty spot beside Dad. He had a nap this afternoon and his eyes look wide awake behind his glasses.

"Catch any criminals this week?" I ask, tucking myself under his arm. I like hearing about all the exciting stuff that happens at his work. Except for the crazy hours, I think he has the coolest job in the world. He carries a walkie-talkie and wears a badge and a uniform and everything.

He grins at me from behind his shaggy beard. "Sure did."

"Tell us," I demand. Jack turns to listen while Bobcat glares at me from his lap. I stick out my tongue at him. And then I feel dumb because, well, he's a cat.

"It happened last night," Dad says. "I was sitting at my desk, manning the cameras and minding my own business, when one of my monitors went dark. At first, I wasn't worried. I figured it was just a camera malfunction — those happen every now and then. But when I leaned in for a closer look, I saw something strange. There were a couple of folds on the screen."

He pauses here for dramatic effect. I give a tug on his pinky finger.

"What does that mean?"

"It means, Daisy, that someone had covered up the security camera. On purpose."

My stomach does a flip when I hear that. I sit up and face him. "What'd you do?"

He scratches the underside of his bearded chin. "Well, technically I wasn't supposed to leave the monitors. But the mall had been closed for over an hour and nothing else was going on. So I asked Dave to take over for me and went out to investigate. The camera in question was overlooking the food court, which isn't far from the security desk."

"You went alone?" Jack asks, crunching down hard on a popcorn kernel. The crunch is so loud, it sounds like a branch snapping. Bob jumps off his lap and runs to hide under the couch.

"What did you find?" I ask.

"I found the thief, of course. He was right there behind the counter of the sandwich kiosk. Caught him red-handed."

Jack's eyes are so wide, they look like a couple of Ping-Pong balls. "He was stealing from the cash register?"

"Actually, he was eating a leftover turkey panini."

"A panini?" I snort. "Why wasn't he trying to steal money?"

Dad's still scratching his beard. I guess maybe that helps him think better. "I can't say for sure. But from the look of him, I don't think he'd sat down to a good meal in a long time."

He pauses again and I take a second to imagine

how the thief must have looked to make Dad say something like that. Skinny. Dirty. Raggedy clothes. Sick, maybe. My stomach does a different kind of flip.

"Did he have a gun?" Jack asks.

"No," Dad says, shaking his head. "My guess is that this guy must have hidden himself in the mall as it was shutting down so he could go after the food. It was his old sweatshirt that was covering the security camera."

"So what did you do to him?"

Dad stops scratching and peers at us over the top of his glasses. "What would you two have done if you were me?"

My brain twitches. Dad loves testing us with hard questions. I glance at my brother to see if I can guess what he's thinking. I've always been curious about the whole twin-connection thing. You know, how scientists believe twins can hear each other's thoughts and feel each other's emotions? Last summer, I was kind of obsessed with quizzing Jack on it. I was always asking him if he knew what colour I was picturing or what number I had in my head. He almost never got it right. But then again, he doesn't believe those scientists anyway, so he might have just been messing with me. Colours and numbers aside, I think the scientists are definitely on to something. Because there have been times, totally random moments, where it feels like we can read each other's mind.

Jack puts his hand up, like he's in school. "I'd call the police," he says really fast, like it's obvious.

Ugh. That's not what I was thinking. At all.

"No way, that's too harsh," I say, trying the scratch thing on my own chin. "I think I'd make him pay the store back for the stolen panini."

Jack laughs at my answer. "That's dumb. If the guy had the money to pay, why would he be stealing?"

I glance back at Dad. From the look on his face, I have a feeling both our answers are wrong.

"So what did you do?"

"Well, first thing I told the man that he was trespassing on private property and would have to leave. Then I escorted him to the security desk, took my dinner out of the fridge, and gave it to him. Dave gave him his jacket, then we both walked him to the exit."

"What?" Jack says. "But he was trying to rob the mall."

"Only because he was hungry. I don't think a person should be punished for that. Do you?"

This time, the answer comes easily. "No," I say, shaking my head hard. "Definitely not."

Jack's shaking his head too.

"Remember," Dad says, "it's important to be kind whenever possible — and it's always possible. Do you know who said that?"

Jack closes his eyes and groans. "The Dalai Lama," he says, flopping back in his chair. "You've told us that one a bazillion times already."

I should probably mention that Dad has a thing about teaching famous quotes to Jack and me. I guess he thinks we'll grow up to be important if we know what other important people used to talk about. Pretty corny, right? Last weekend, it was all about Gandhi. And the week before that, a dude named Winston Churchill. But the DL is definitely his favourite. He likes to quote him. A lot.

"Is that story true, Nate?" I ask, studying his face. "Did you really give the thief your dinner?"

"What do you think, Daisy?"

I stare into his eyes — really deep so I find all the colours. Beneath the blue, there are sprinkles of green and brown and purple. And beneath the sprinkles, there's a little spark of gold, so tiny, you can only see it if you look close enough. That little golden spark must reach all the way down to his heart because every time I find it, my own heart feels bigger.

"I think you're a great security guard," I say, cuddling back up under his arm. I run my fingers through the ends of his shaggy beard. These days, it looks more grey than brown. Plus it's in bad need of a trim. It's way too tickly when he kisses me good night. And he gets crumbs stuck in it at every meal. I've heard Mom asking him to trim it, but Dad doesn't care about how a thing looks. Whether it's overgrown beards or overgrown vines, it doesn't matter to him.

Just between you and me, I happen to know our house wasn't always a jungle. I found a photo from the year my parents bought it, way back when they were first married. The vines must have been just newly planted because you can barely even see them. I don't know what shocked me more about the photo: seeing the bare brick and clean windows of our home, or seeing how different Mom and Dad looked back then. They were so young, it's hard to believe the picture was only taken fifteen years ago.

Mom likes telling the story of how fast the vines took over after she and Dad moved in, and how our house is a living monument to the power of Mother Nature. Whenever I suggest that maybe we could trim the vines back a bit, she looks at me like I have two heads. At least in the old days, they used to keep the windows clear of leaves. But then Jack got sick and suddenly gardening didn't matter so much anymore. And then Dad got switched onto the night shift and started sleeping all day. And Mom had to stop working for a long time to take care of Jack. After that, she went full-time at the restaurant to help pay all the bills.

Mom wanders back into the room, dressed in her favourite pair of rainbow pyjamas. She stumbles over the laundry basket filled with yesterday's wash. "What kind of stories are you filling these young heads with, Nate?" she asks, pushing the basket out of the way with her bare foot.

Dad gives me a squeezy hug. "Just telling them about some of my exciting misadventures at work."

I'm about to retell the story about the hungry thief when Jack starts coughing. Mom dashes to the kitchen for a glass of water, then perches on the arm of Jack's chair, patting his back with one hand and feeling his forehead with the other as he sips from the glass. The room goes quiet.

"I'm fine," Jack says as soon as he catches his breath. "It was just a popcorn kernel. Will you guys quit looking at me like that?" He smiles to show us he's okay.

I let out the breath I didn't know I'd been holding. Jack's in remission (which is a fancy way to say he's a lot better now). In fact, if you met him on the street, you'd never guess he was ever sick. But the doctors warned us it could come back. So to me and my parents, he's like a sleeping volcano. We're always on the lookout for signs he's going to erupt again.

I don't know what I'd do if that happened.

"Sorry, Jack-Kerouac," Mom says, ruffling his hair. "Just want to be sure." This time when she reaches for the popcorn bowl, he lets her take it away. "Anybody want a glass of root beer?"

"I do," Jack says.

I stick out my tongue and pretend to gag. "No, thanks." Mom's root beer is homemade and healthy. Of course. It's made with real roots she digs up from the backyard. She and Jack call it "a glass of health." I call it nasty mud water.

Sitting up, I give Dad's shoulder a poke. "Can you

walk me over to Willow's house now? We're having a sleepover tonight."

"I guess so," he says, grunting under his breath as he pulls himself off the couch. I'd rather stay too, but I don't say it out loud. Willow and I both wanted to have our last sleepover of the school year at my house, but her parents said no. She's leaving next week for overnight camp and they said they want her in her own bed until then. She super-begged and puppy-faced them like crazy to change their minds. But they wouldn't budge. Willow wasn't happy about that. She's never come out and admitted it but the girl's seriously obsessed with my house. When we were younger, she used to call it Jungleland — like it was some kind of amusement park. She told me once that she feels safe here, like she's inside a secret fortress. I guess it's easy to forget the rest of the world exists when you're here. The vines block pretty much everything from the outside world. The only noises left are the birds and the scampering of animal feet over the roof. And the leaves, of course. When the wind gets up, they start whispering and sighing. Sometimes it sounds like the house is talking. Or breathing. Or both.

Sometimes I wonder if it actually is.

Willow doesn't like spending time at her own home these days. Her parents are out almost every night. Which means she's left on her own a lot. Not that she's scared. But I guess it can get pretty lonely in that big empty house. At least at my place, all we have to worry about is the darkness. And the bugs. And Bobcat. And the snakes.

I mentioned those, right?

The best part about sleeping at Willow's house is her bed. It's so big, you have to climb a stepstool to get into it. And so poofy, you feel like you're buried inside a giant marshmallow. When we sleep at my house, it's thin blankets on a hard floor with a side of ants. But she never, ever complains.

The second-best part about sleeping at Willow's house is that we get to eat as much junk food as we want. And her kitchen cupboards are fully stocked. As soon as I get there, we grab a load of snacks, go straight to her room, and flip on her iPod. Willow's bedroom is massive. And it's painted bright turquoise, like a swimming pool on a sunny day. Whenever I'm here, I feel like I've gone on holiday.

I pull the house folder out of my bag and open

it up on the bed. Back when we were nine, Willow and I decided that we're going to be roommates when we grow up. We agreed that getting a husband and having to kiss him like they do in the movies when it looks like they're trying to swallow each other's face isn't something either of us wants to do. Ever. So we pinky-swore we'd never get boyfriends and we're going to build a big house together when we turn twenty-one and be roommates forever. The folder's full of drawings and pictures of what we want our house to look like. Willow wants a movie theatre and a bowling alley and a lake or ocean so she can go swimming any time she wants to. She also wants a waterfall and a goldfish pond in the front yard, and two hammocks side by side in the back. That's all fine with me. The only thing I want is for it to look normal. And lots of windows in every room. No curtains covering them. No vines either. Oh yeah . . . and a flagpole, just like at an official camp. And, of course, an extra bedroom for Jack. If there's still a Jack. But he's the only boy we're going to allow in.

Tonight, Willow announces that she wants to add a Ferris wheel to the plans. "Just as huge as the one near the London Bridge," she says, showing me a picture she tore out of a travel magazine. We stay up way past midnight, chewing on sour belts and trying to decide where we're going to put it. We have a fun time, but Willow seems distracted. Like her thoughts have taken a vacation to Florida and left her body behind.

"Okay, so would you rather squeeze lemon juice into a paper cut," I ask, pulling the covers up over my ear, "or stub your baby toe on a porcupine?"

"Ouch . . . um, I'll take the paper cut," Willow says.

"Yeah, me too."

She folds her pillow in half and yawns. "My turn. Would you rather live where there's no summer? Or give up ice cream forever?"

I don't even hesitate. "I love ice cream way too much to ever give it up."

"Not me. Ice cream gets the boot. I couldn't live without summer."

I could. If giving up summer meant she wouldn't go away anymore.

"Willow?" I whisper.

"Yeah?" she whispers back.

"I wish you didn't have to go to camp."

"It's only seven weeks."

"Gonna miss you madly," I say in the split second before falling asleep.

I'm not sure, but I think I hear her say: "Don't."

I end up spending a good chunk of our last week together trying to figure out what that means.

Chapter 5

I wake up this morning to the usual chirp-fest outside my window. *Something important's happening today,* I think, dragging myself out from under a heavy sleep. Squinting open my right eye, I peer around my room, trying to remember what it is. The sunlight shining through the leaves outside my window is casting a shimmering green light over my walls. For just a few seconds, it makes me feel like I'm inside a giant glass marble. Prying open my other eye, I stretch my fingertips up to the ceiling and inhale a deep breath of morning air.

I think today's going to be a good day, I tell myself. Behind the chirps, the vines outside my window are shivering in the breeze. Sounds like three little words, whispered over and over again: *Go to schoo-ool. Go to schoo-ool.*

That's when I remember what day it *actually* is. And now I wish I could tell those stupid birds to stop singing.

Hopping out of bed, I march across my room and clear the activity board with one angry swipe. Jungle-camp is officially closed for the season. That thought makes my stomach start swirling so bad, I have to sit down on my bed and put my head between my knees until the pukey feeling goes away. I try thinking about strawberries and rainbows and big fluffy clouds floating high in a true blue sky. But nothing helps.

Have you ever felt like someone's scribbled all over your insides with a fine tip Sharpie? That's how I feel right now and I want everyone to know it, so I dress in all black from head to toe. Black is the only colour for this kind of day. I don't even care that I look like a miniature vampire. I don't even care that we're in the middle of a heat wave and my school's not air conditioned. Because today's the last day of school. Which means Willow leaves for her other camp this afternoon. Every summer, she goes to Camp Couchikoo for seven whole weeks. And every summer, I stay home and count the minutes until she gets back.

I head downstairs for breakfast, relieved that Mom had to leave early for work so I can finish off my secret box of Lucky Charms. I'm pretty sure it's the only thing my pukey stomach can handle right now and I know I'm going to need lots of energy to survive this day.

When I'm done eating, I wait for Jack in the front hallway. Resting my head against the wall, I pull the strings of my black hoodie tight around my face.

"Are you coming?" I yell through the mouth hole.

A minute later he comes charging down the stairs, two steps at a time. He's dressed in red shorts and his favourite Toronto Raptors jersey. He got it a few years ago, but it's still a couple sizes too big for him. The Raptors game was one of those sick-kid-wish-fulfillment things and our whole family got to ride down to the stadium in a limo and sit courtside and meet the team and everything. Jack loves basketball. He wants to be an NBA player when he grows up.

If he grows up.

When he reaches the bottom of the stairs, he pauses. "Why are you dressed like a ninja?" he asks, pointing at my clothes. "It's not Halloween."

I sigh. "I know what month it is, thanks," I say, picking up my backpack and hiking it over my shoulder. "FYI, these are traditional funerary colours."

"You're going to a funeral today?" He pats his hands over his chest and arms. "Wait . . . am I a ghost?"

Grinning wide enough so I can see the empty spot in the back of his mouth where he lost a molar last week, he waggles his fingers high in the air and yells "Boo" so loud, it blows the bangs off my face.

"Shut up, dooberdog," I say. But I can't help smiling.

"Seriously, you can't go to school like that. You're going to roast."

"I don't care," I say, pulling open the front door. "Grappa wears black all summer long and you don't bug him about it. Besides, it's not that hot anyway."

At least it's not in our house. The thick layer of vines somehow manages to keep the rooms coolish in the summer. And warmish in the winter. Mom says the vines give our house insulation. I secretly think it's one of the reasons why Dad let them take over. He'll do anything to save money on the electricity bill.

"Whatever. But everyone's going to laugh at you," Jack warns.

"Told you, I don't care," I reply, trying to sound tough. We head outside and I let out a yelp when a thick wall of heat slams into me. It's so hot I'm dripping before we even reach the sidewalk. Now all I can imagine are the rings of sweat that are gonna start soaking through my armpits.

Charming.

Okay, so maybe I do care. Just a bit.

I stop walking. "Go ahead without me. I'll catch up."

Jack stops too. "Maybe I should wait," he says, glancing up and down the sidewalk.

My brother likes to think of himself as my personal bodyguard. Especially this year, after we got split into different classes for the first time in our lives. I can practically feel the worry oozing out of him. Not sure if that's a twin thing or not.

I give him a gentle shove. "Go to school, Toe," I say in my strictest yeah-I-*am*-the-boss-of-you voice.

He hesitates. "Do you at least want me to tell your teacher you might be late?"

"No. Don't worry, I'll be fine," I add, dashing back into the house before he can say another word.

Up in my room, I peel off my funeral wear and change into a faded blue T-shirt and jean shorts. I race back outside, hoping there's still time to catch up with Jack. But I'm not even ten steps out the front door when something cold and wet hits me from behind. I squeal from the shock. The water's like a punch.

"Ooops, didn't see you there," says a gravelly voice. I spin around to see old Mrs. Pitt standing in front of the rose bushes. She's wearing knee-high rubber boots, a pink track suit and a wide-brimmed straw hat. Her guilty garden hose is clutched tightly in one hand, a plastic water bottle in the other.

"You soaked me," I say, shaking the freezing drops of water from my arms. Is that a hint of a smile on her red-lipsticked mouth? This lady's been out to get our family for years. Yeah, she totally did it on purpose.

"So sorry, dear," she replies, with a phony *tsk-tsk*. "But maybe if your parents would prune back that house of yours, you'da seen me standing here." She takes a slurpy sip from her planet-polluting bottle.

I'm about to ask how she can see anything under that dumb hat. And why she and her husband are always so mean and grumpy. And why she hates kids so much. But I swallow the words down before they can come out.

Be the Dalai Lama, Daisy.

I clench my teeth into a tight smile, searching for my inner DL "Have a nice day, Mrs. Pitt," I say. Turning around stiffly, I head back inside.

"Your family has no respect for the rest of this neighbourhood!" she calls after me. "Be warned, Karl and I are planning on filing another complaint."

Ignoring her, I close the front door behind me and run up the stairs to my room. On the way, I consider waking Dad and telling him what just happened. But in the end, I decide against it. The Pitts have been filing complaints about our family for years. Fact is, the Jungle's not breaking any laws. Dad explained it all to me a hundred times. As long as the vines aren't growing over their property line, there's nothing the Pitts or anyone else can do about it.

I tear through my closet for fresh clothes because now I'm getting changed for the *third* time this morning. Good thing I remembered to bring the laundry in, or I'd be forced to raid Jack's closet. I race all the way to school, stopping for only a couple of seconds to help Mr. Lee with his garbage cans. By the time I finally make it to the schoolyard, the second bell is already ringing. I sprint straight to class. Willow waves at me as I slide into my seat.

"Why's your hair wet?" she whispers.

Is it? I run a hand over the back of my head. "Tell you later."

"Weeeee-eeeeed's laaaaa-aaaaate!" whines a high-pitched voice from the back of the room. I don't turn to look, but I'd bet every dollar in my piggy bank that it's

Shana Birkin. Shana's the meanest girl in sixth grade and she's been on my case about the Jungle since the day of that party. It was a long time ago, but from what I remember, she was the first kid to start screaming.

I pretend to ignore her. That's usually the fastest way to make her stop. But it's the last day of school and kids are feeling reckless and a few seconds later the monkey noises start. Just one at first but it must be contagious because soon enough a chorus of *ooo-ooo-ooos* and *aaa-aaa-aaas* are bouncing like super balls around the room. My stomach starts feeling pukey again. I lean forward in my seat, trying to make eye contact with Ms. Tushinsky. But she's staring at her desk and won't look up. Her shoulders are slumped and her head is resting in her hands like she's ready to go back to bed. It's the last day of school. She looks like she's already on vacation.

A second later, something hits the back of my chair. I spin around in my seat to see what it is.

A banana. Squished and spotted and curled up on the floor beside my desk. How cliché.

My face burns. I know for a fact this wouldn't be happening if I lived in a normal house like everyone else.

Around me, snorts of laughter mingle with the monkey calls. Somewhere above all the noise, I can just make out Willow's voice.

"Daisy? You okay?"

I shake my head.

A few seconds later, there's a scuffling of shoes beside me. I look over to see Willow climbing on top of her chair. Her face is a thundercloud and her hands are balled into fists at her sides like she's ready for a fight. She brings her purple sneaker crashing down on the seat with a mighty stomp that cuts through all the chaos.

"Hey, meatballs! Shut up or I'll fart! I mean it. I've got a big one ready to go. I'm warning you, it'll be silent but deadly."

The monkey calls fade into stunned silence. Willow winks at me as she climbs back down. *Thanks,* I say with my eyes. She nods and gives me the thumbs-up. Looking relieved, Ms. Tushinsky picks up the attendance sheet and starts checking off names. I'm not sure why, because it's the last day of school and so attendance can't really matter.

Can it?

"Daisy Fisher?"

"Here." The word crawls from my mouth, tiny as an ant.

Hunching down in my seat, so far my chin hits the desk, I watch the second hand sweep across the clock. And wonder how I'm ever going to survive the next seven weeks without Willow.

Why do I have the feeling this could be the start of the worst summer ever?

Chapter 6

"Yoo-hoo, Daisy? You awake?"

It's Mom. Her voice sounds sludgy, like it's covered in a layer of Cheez Whiz. I roll over and pull the blanket over my head.

"Nomph."

Her cool hand pats my back, tickles my neck, gives my shoulder a gentle shake. I push my face into my pillow and squeeze my eyes shut, trying so hard to hold on to the delicious sleep that's quickly slipping away. The only decent thing about summer vacation is sleeping in. I'm not getting up till I'm good and ready.

School's been out for a week now and each day's been more boring than the last. It seems like every kid I know is busy with programs or camp or off on vacation. Every kid but me and Jack. Mom and Dad don't have the extra money for stuff like that. At least

I've had Jack for company, even though he doesn't want to do anything except read comic books and shoot hoops in the driveway. Yesterday I tried to recruit him for Junglecamp. But he wasn't interested.

"Come on, it'll be fun!" I said. "We can make it a basketball theme day if you want."

"You know it's not *real* camp."

"Not very DL, Master Toe," I said, crossing my arms in front of my chest. "And PS, yes it is!"

He tucked the basketball under his arm and turned to look at me. His usual smiling face was dragging. "No, it's *not,*" he snapped. "It can't be a real camp without actual campers! Even Mom and Dad think it's lame. Last night I heard them talking and they said the only reason you made it up is because you're searching for structure and order in a house of chaos."

Whoa. For a second, I was speechless. "Who pooped in your oat bran this morning?" I snapped back. I'd never, ever seen my brother so cranky before. Well, except for that time four years ago when he stubbed his big toe on the coffee table leg and whined and cried and grumped about it for two hours straight. (Which, FYI, is the short version of how he earned his nickname.)

I retaliated the only way I knew how. Slapping the ball out from under his arm, I aimed at the hoop and hurled it into the air. We watched the ball toilet-bowl around the rim for a few seconds before finally falling through.

"Fluke!" he growled, grabbing the ball back.

"Sorry not sorry," I said, turning back to the house. *What's wrong with him?* I remember thinking, as I walked away.

"Rabbit?" Mom's voice is getting clearer now. I can smell sweet almond milk on her morning breath. She must have had coffee already.

"No. Goway."

"Sorry, but we're leaving. I just want you to know."

"What?" I squint open my eyes. Mom's sitting beside me on the bed. She's wearing cut-off jean shorts, a faded pink T-shirt and her lucky dolphin earrings. A neon-yellow bandana is tied over her hair. For a second I think I might still be dreaming. "Who's leaving?" I mumble. "Why aren't you dressed for work?"

"Nate and I are taking Jack out this morning. Hopefully we won't be too long."

She reaches out to tuck the blanket around my legs,

fanning the ends to make a fishtail at my feet. Just like she used to do when I was younger. *Now you're a mermaid, Daisy,* she would say. And then she'd tickle my arm and tell me a story of a little girl who lived in a seaweed house under the waves.

By now, I'm fully awake. I rise up on an elbow and rub some crust out of my eye.

"Where are you guys going?"

She picks at a ball of fluff on my blanket. Her fingernails are chewed so short, it hurts to look at them. "Jack's got an appointment downtown . . ." She bites down on her lower lip, like she's struggling to stop herself from saying more. Normally, Jack going to an appointment is no big deal. He gets check-ups all the time. But something about Mom's face isn't right. Her smile looks stiff and strange — like someone's glued it to her mouth. My throat goes dry. I try to swallow but I can't. It feels like my tongue's coated with sand.

"What kind of appointment?" I croak.

"Oh, Daisy . . ." Her voice is light and easy. But that weird frozen smile is still stuck to her face. Something's up. She covers my hand with hers. "It's just one of those follow-up visits. Dr. Ip wants to do a test or two. It's really nothing to worry about. Okay?"

I know she's still talking but it doesn't matter 'cause at this point I've stopped listening. My heart is pounding a wild drumbeat in my ears.

I close my eyes as a flood of awful memories comes over me. Teams of whispering doctors in their cool white coats. The sickening bleached smell of green hospital rooms. Needles and pills and barf and Jack all thin and pale and bald and hooked up to a million tubes. Hearing him moan in his sleep. Listening for his breath and ready to scream for help the moment it disappeared. Mom and Dad crying but covering it up whenever I walked into the room and pretending to be strong because they were trying to hide how scared they really were.

I always knew.

No, no, no. Jack can't be sick again. He can't.

Suddenly it feels like I can't get enough air into my lungs. Is there a maple tree pollinating nearby? I thought maple season was over.

"Here," Mom says, handing me the puffer I keep on my nightstand. I flip off the cap and suck in some medicine. I hold my breath for ten seconds then let it out slowly.

Better.

"Okay now?" Mom asks, rubbing her hand up and down my back.

"Frieda?" I hear Dad's voice calling from downstairs. "We better go!"

"Daisy?" she asks. "Did you hear what I said?"

"Yeah." I nod as I pull in another deep breath. "I'm fine."

She glances at her watch. "Oops, we're going to be late." She jumps up and pats herself down, searching for her keys. As soon as she finds them, she turns her head and blows a quick kiss over her shoulder. "Be sure to feed the chickens, okay? Toodle-oo."

"Wait!"

But she's already out the door.

I fall back onto my pillow with a flump. Guess I know why Jack was so grouchy yesterday.

Schnitzel. This is so bad.

I don't want to think about any of that right now. I grab a pen off my nightstand and flip to a fresh page in my journal. Maybe today's the day I'll start writing my book. Did I mention that I'm going to be a writer when I grow up? Dad says I'll be great at it because I love books and stories. Also because I have an overactive imagination. I hold the pen steady and stare at the blank page for a few minutes, waiting for the words to come. I wait for a really long time but the only thing I can think of writing is a letter to Willow at camp. So that's what I do.

Dear Willow,
How's camp? Everything sucks here. You know how I was going to be a paperback writer like in the Beatles song? Well, it's not happening anymore because I have no clue what to write. Not one word. And don't even try to be nice and tell me it's called "writer's block" because that only counts if you're a real writer (and I'm pretty sure you officially have to have written at least one word to be a real writer).

It hailed last weekend. The ice was as big as grapes and it came down so hard it was bouncing off the grass. It was cool, except there's a new leak in my ceiling and this one's over my bed, so when the hail turned to rain later that afternoon, the water dripped all over my pillow. It might have been okay if the raindrops bounced, but they didn't. They just soaked in and made my pillow soggy. And so I have to remember to sleep with my head at the foot of my bed, just in case it starts to rain in the middle of the night. And I'm so scared because I think Jack is sick again. This is turning out to be the worst summer of my life.

Yesterday's corny Dad-quote was: Misery loves company. Some dead guy named John Ray said it a million years ago. It made me think of you. I'm miserable. Are you miserable too? I miss you so much it makes me nauseous.

(My stomach growls just as I write that part, so I cross out "nauseous" and put in "hungry.")

Please, please, please write back soon!
Love,
Daisy

P.S. Bob got off his leash yesterday. Jack and I found him in the yard across the street. He was stalking Mrs. Smythe's new Maltipoo. Luckily, we caught him and carried him home before there was bloodshed. Mrs. Smythe was so grateful she gave us one of her prize zucchinis. Jack blended it up for a smoothie.

P.P.S. What would you rather: A slow death being squeezed in the grip of a giant boa constrictor? Or having to drink a zucchini smoothie?

I rip out the letter and fold it up for mailing. Closing the journal, I pull on a T-shirt and head downstairs for breakfast. But after a quick search of the kitchen, all I can find to eat is some leftover brown rice, plain yogourt and a bunch of nearly black bananas. Barf. I wonder if there are any more Lucky Charms in the basement hiding spot. I think I remember Dad saying he bought another box last week. Problem is, I hate going down there. Our basement is dark and cold and sinister — a scene straight out of a scary movie.

My stomach growls again, louder than ever — like it's telling me to suck it up and go find some food. With a sigh, I tiptoe over to the stairs. The rusty hinges shriek as I pull open the door. I peer down into the long black hole, turning my ear to the darkness and listening for noises from the creepy things that live there. The basement is where really big bugs hang out. A long time ago, there used to be mice down there too, but Mom and Dad promise they're all gone now (although they won't tell us how they got rid of them, and I'm pretty sure it wasn't "catch and release"). When we were little, Jack and I used to dare each other to go down to the bottom and stand there for a count of a hundred. Jack could do it, but I never made it past ten before racing back to the safety of upstairs.

I wait for a really long time — long enough to let a coat of nail polish set. (The regular kind, not the quick-dry.) There's nothing but the sound of air humming through the vents.

Okay, Daze. You can do this.

Nervously, I make my way down. *Flop, flop, flop* go my bare feet on the smooth wooden stairs. *Thup, thup, thup* goes the pulse in my ears. The air down here smells earthy and damp. And it's cold. And so dark, by the time I'm halfway down I can't see my hands anymore. The rest of the Jungle can get pretty shadowy, but our basement is like pitch-black permanent midnight. Once I get to the bottom, I hop quickly across the cool cement floor to the spot where I know the metal chain hangs from the ceiling bulb. Okay, I know I'm not supposed to turn a light on this early in the day. But this is an emergency. I know Dad would understand. I yelp at the feel of baby vines curling around my ankles, certain they're trying to grab on to me so they can keep me down here forever. I wrap one arm around my head to protect my ears (just in case of giant earwigs). With my free hand I feel around for the chain. I pull once, twice, three times. But there's no light. I yank it hard one more time and the whole chain comes loose, lashing my hand as it breaks away from the bulb with a snap.

Drizzle.

I broke it.

Now I'm standing here like a dummy, hungry and scared out of my wits, with a busted chain dangling from my fist. Did something just scurry over my big toe? I jump and scream, terrified it's a monster bug or a mouse or something even worse. Afraid to stand still for too long, I hop from one foot to the next while I try to figure out what to do.

Don't freak out, Daze. Just go grab the cereal and get out of here.

The chain drops to the floor with a clank. I take two steps in the direction of the pantry but freeze before I go any farther. I just heard a noise. It came from upstairs.

"Frieda, Nate? Jack?" I yell. But there's no way they're back from their appointment this early. Now there's a freaky rattling sound that sets the hairs on the back of my neck on end.

"Bob?" I whisper, hoping, wishing, praying it's just the dumb cat playing a trick on me.

The rattle comes again, quickly followed by a sharp bang. It's coming from the front door.

Someone's trying to break in.

This is the part when I forget how to breathe.

What do I do? What do I do? Hide? Scream? Maybe I should call 911? But there's no phone down here.

I turn my eyes to the glowing rectangle of light at the top of the staircase. My mind races as I struggle to pull some air into my lungs.

Do I have enough time to run up there and grab a phone before the burglars make it inside?

Above me, I hear a pair of heavy footsteps

trudging across the hardwood floor. My heart flies into my throat.

You're out of time, Daze! Do something!

A second later, I hear a voice screaming.

"Get out of my house right now! I've called the police and they're going to be here any second!"

Yeah, that was totally me.

The footsteps stop. A shadowy figure appears at the top of the stairs. It's shaped like a man. I scream again, so loud my ears ring.

"Daisy?" the shape says, clomping down the stairs toward me. "Is that you?"

Chapter 7

I stop screaming. My body sags with relief.

"Grappa!" I say, throwing myself into his arms. "What are you doing here?"

He drops his key chain and hugs me back. "Sorry I scared you. Your mom asked me to come spend the day while they're out with Jack. Didn't she tell you?"

"I don't know," I say, remembering back to this morning's conversation. "Frieda was talking, but I wasn't really listening."

Grappa snorts and ruffles my hair. "Only twelve, but turning into a proper teenager already! Right. You okay now? Let's get going."

Scooping up his keys, he takes my hand and leads me back up the stairs.

"But I haven't had my breakfast yet."

"No worries, kid. I'm taking you out to eat. It's so

darn dark in this house, I couldn't find a fork if my life depended on it."

"Are we going to ride on your tricycle?"

He turns around and winks. "Does a pig say oink? I brought your favourite helmet too."

Before we go any farther, I should probably explain a little bit about my Grappa. He's not exactly your typical cardigan-wearing, golf-loving grandfather. Grappa is way cool. All his clothes are black or leather (preferably both), he wears his curly grey hair down to his shoulders and he has a huge collection of skull jewellery that he switches up every day. He also has an apartment full of pets and drives a motor-trike (that's a motorcycle with three wheels) everywhere he goes. Grappa's the bomb. My brother and I want to be just like him when we grow up.

"Did Frieda tell you anything about Jack's appointment?" I ask. We're outside on the driveway now and he's fastening the strap on my favourite helmet — the one with the purple skull painted on the side.

"Yeah, she said it's nothing to worry about. So I'm not going to. And neither should you." He winks again before popping on his sunglasses. "Hey, you were pretty brave back there. Did you really think I was a burglar?"

My cheeks burn with embarrassment. "Nah. I was just trying to trick you."

He gives my helmet a pat. "Good job, kid."

We climb onto his trike and Grappa revs the engine good and loud. I hold my breath as gas fumes rise up around us and wrap my arms around his round tummy. That's when I spot Mr. Pitt on the other side of the rose bushes. He's standing in his driveway, wrestling with a big grey suitcase in the trunk of his precious car — an electric-blue antique Chevrolet from the olden days. He's always out on his driveway cleaning it with a bottle of organic shampoo and a sheepskin glove. Dad says the car is a classic. Mom says it's Mr. Pitt's "baby."

Right now, his face is turning bright red and the top of his bald head is covered in a film of sweat as he tries to keep the edges of the suitcase from scratching his "baby."

Are the Pitts going away on a trip? My heart does a happy dance at the thought. *With a bit of luck, maybe they'll be gone all summer!*

"Need some help with that, neighbour?" Grappa yells over the roar of the engine.

"No, Grappa, don't talk to that guy," I hiss in his ear. "He's the enemy. Remember?"

Mr. Pitt glares in our direction. The scowl on his face is very clearly telling us to mind our own beeswax.

"Not from you!" he grunts, turning his attention back to the stubborn suitcase.

Grappa glances over his shoulder at me. "Who pooped in his oat bran?"

"It's us, not you. Don't take it personally," I reply, holding tight as we take off down the driveway. "He hates kids. And vines."

"Well then, just remember what Abe Lincoln used to say." He's yelling now so I can hear him.

"What's that?" I ask, leaning in as we turn a corner onto Main Street.

"The best way to destroy an enemy," he yells over the rush of wind, "is to make him a friend. Your dad told me that one last week."

Well, that's just ridonkulous. I try to tell him so, but all I get is a mouthful of bugs.

After breakfast, Grappa and I drive down to the lake and take a ferry to the islands. We have a sushi picnic and he tells me about his new girlfriend and teaches me some of his favourite swears. They're mostly the same kind of words I've heard the older kids use at the park, but I don't want to hurt his feelings so I pretend to be impressed. Like I told you already, Mom and Dad don't have too many rules and they don't really care what Jack and I say, so long as we're not hurting anyone. I guess maybe that's why we don't swear like everyone else. Besides, it's way more fun to make up your own. So I decide to teach Grappa some of my favourites. He'd never heard any of them before.

"That's because they're originals," I say.

"But those aren't real swears," he says with that pretzely know-it-all kind of smile grown-ups like to use.

"They are. Cross my heart and eat a pie," I say. "Try them out sometime. You'll see."

"Okay, I'll let you know how it goes."

After lunch we rent paddle boats and race them around the island. But Grappa's watch is broken so we kinda lose track of the day. By the time we get home, it's after dinner. I'm positive we're going to be in trouble but nobody seems to care that we're late. They don't even notice that my nose got sunburned from being outside all day without a hat. I breeze through the living room and go looking for Jack. I'm itching to ask how his appointment went. But he's in his room and doesn't want to come out. Not even for a minute to say hi. When I go to ask Mom about the appointment, she just says, "It went fine." When I ask what that means, she gives me another of those "it's nothing to worry about" lines.

Are those new wrinkles on her forehead?

So I stop asking questions. Because suddenly, I'm not exactly sure I want to hear the answers.

*

Today Mom's back at work and Jack's all sunshine, ice cream and rainbow sprinkles again and I'm so relieved, I grab him and hug him tight until he says ow and I have to let him go. I don't even want to bring the subject back up. I try really hard to stop myself. But in the end, curiosity gets me. Like always.

"How was yesterday?" I ask, cornering him in the kitchen while he's making a smoothie.

"Boring."

"What took you guys so long?"

He shrugs as he dumps a mushy banana and some frozen fruit into the blender. "You know how doctors are."

"Did you see Dr. Ip?"

"Yeah."

I drum my fingers on the counter while he ducks his head into the fridge. When he comes out, he's holding the container of plain yogourt.

"So, spill. What did he say?"

Jack shrugs again and rummages in the drawer for a spoon. "Just wizzly doctor stuff. I wasn't really listening."

Okay, now I'm getting nervous.

"Just be straight with me."

"I am."

"You can tell me anything, Toe."

"There's nothing to tell."

I stomp my foot like a two-year-old. "Come on, Jack!" I say in my I'm-older-by-eight-minutes-and-you-have-to-listen-to-me voice.

He puts the yogourt container down with a sigh.

"Laze," he says, shaking his head.

"Yeah?"

"I know what you're doing." He raises one eyebrow, like a scheming mad scientist. It's one of those random twin ESP moments where I know he can read my mind — which isn't fair because, as hard as I'm trying, I can't seem to read his. "It's nothing to worry about. I promise. Okay?"

He's smiling like normal, but it's not exactly connecting with his eyes. And his voice is prickly, like a warning to drop the subject. So I do.

"Okay," I huff, holding up my hands and backing out of the kitchen. But it's a lie. 'Cause I know something's up. Something's up and nobody will talk about it.

And now I'm more worried than ever.

When I find a postcard from Willow in the mailbox later in the morning, I forget my worries for a minute and do a pirouette right there on the porch. On the front of the card is a sunset scene of Lake Couchikoo. Cute, right? I flip it over to read the rest. That's when I stop spinning.

> *Hey Daze,*
> *How's Jungleland? Are the raspberries ready? Don't be sitting around missing me all day!*
> *See you in a few weeks.*
> *xo*
> *W*

Okay, so there's only *so* much room on a postcard. Plus Willow's not exactly Shakespeare. Still, this letter is kind of lame. She's been gone for nine whole days and all I got is twenty-five words? (And that's only with me being generous and counting *x*, *o* and *w* as actual words.)

Pushing the postcard between the pages of my book, I head to the backyard, pick a handful of raspberries, and find a spot to sit in the shade of the chestnut tree. I roll each berry around in my mouth for a few seconds before smashing it on my tongue. The book I'm reading is about a girl who lives in New York City. She's twelve years old like me and she's also got a twin brother and a cat. Only her cat's cute and cuddly and her brother's not a ticking time bomb. It's supposed to be a real-life story, but I guess it might as well be a fairy tale because every time there's a problem in the girl's life, she always knows exactly what to do to fix it.

Every.

Fajizzling.

Time.

Halfway through, I close the book with a slap and toss it into the raspberry bushes. Willow's postcard goes with it.

"How stupid do you think I am?" I yell after it.

When I'm an author, I'm going to write a way better book than that.

I get up to go find another book but freeze when I see the Pitts' house. There's a face in one of the windows. And whoever it belongs to is staring right at me. My heart sinks.

Shazbot! They didn't go on vacation after all.

Ducking behind the chestnut tree, I squint through the sunlight to see who it is. It's hard to tell, but the face doesn't look like one I know. It's got big hair and glasses. Or are those binoculars? Why's it staring at me like that? I stare back but it doesn't move. Is it alive? I wave to see if it'll wave back. But instead, it sticks a pink tongue out at me and disappears.

Who was that? My mind spins with possibilities. A spy? A thief? A ghost? A guest? Has the owner of the face been living there all this time? Do the evil Pitts have a prisoner secretly cooped up in their house? I wait to see if the face comes back.

It doesn't.

When Mrs. Pitt comes out into her backyard, I come this close to walking over and asking her about it. But she's carrying her guilty garden hose along with her grudge. And the scowl hanging from her red lips is so menacing, it sends me hurrying back into the safety of the Jungle.

Chapter 8

"Peel!"

Jack and I are at the end of a Bananagrams tournament and I'm beating his butt. Bad. Normally I'm not competitive, but today I'm desperate to win. Loser has to give the winner a foot massage.

I got this.

With a triumphant squeal, I slide my last tile into place and throw my hands in the air. "Bananas!" I whisper-scream, so I don't wake up Dad.

Jack jumps up from his chair and comes to read over my shoulder. "No way," he says, pointing at my maze of letters. "*Orc*'s not an actual word."

"Yeah it is. Read the Hobbit books, Toe."

"And neither is *dipfish*. Or *blooq*! You're cheating."

"Look 'em up if you don't believe me," I say, turning my head so he can't see the fib on my face.

"Fine. This time, I will." He points at me like he's trying to be stern, but I can see the smile tugging at the corners of his mouth. "Don't move."

He runs off to search for a dictionary. I happen to know that Mom sold it at our yard sale last summer, but there's no way I'm going to rub his stinky feet so I'm never going to tell him that. As soon as Jack's out of sight, Bobcat hisses at me from the window ledge. Like he's calling me out for cheating.

"Fine, so I made up a couple of words," I say. "But you're supposed to be on *my* side, you dumb cat. You're *my* pet, remember?"

I guess Jack must have taken him out for a walk this morning because he's still got his red harness on. Maybe that's why he's so grumpy. If I wasn't afraid of losing my hand, I'd consider unfastening it for him.

"If you want something, you gotta ask me nicely," I tell him, wagging my finger in the air a safe distance away from his face. Somewhere along the way my brother got the crazy idea that cats need a daily walk, just like dogs. When Bob was a kitten, Jack used to push him around the neighbourhood in a little blue toy stroller. It was super cute. I think Mom and Dad still have a picture of it in a frame somewhere. Once Bob got bigger, Jack ditched the stroller and taught him how to walk on a leash. Have you ever heard of a cat being walked on a leash? Trust me, it's the most hilarious thing you ever did see. But, hilarious or not, Jack insists on walking Bob every day. Rain or shine. Jack says Bob likes the opportunity to get a bit of exercise. I disagree. I think Bob likes the opportunity to case his next victim.

While I'm waiting for my brother to come back, I glide my hand over the table and scoop up the smooth letter tiles. One by one, I drop them back into the yellow banana bag. *Click, click, click.*

Just as I'm finishing, the doorbell rings. Once, twice, three times.

"Coming," I hiss, running to answer it before Dad wakes up. When I pull the door open, there's a girl standing on our front porch. She's running a hand over one of the stray vines curling down from the awning.

I blink through the sunlight. "Hello?"

The girl looks like she's about my age. She's got frizzy red hair, bushy eyebrows and a face full of freckles. Her eyes are bugging out and her mouth is hanging open like she's just seen a dentist. Or a nest of baby squirrels.

"Incredible," she mumbles, rising onto her tiptoes for a better look.

"Can I help you?" I ask.

The girl's wide eyes finally land on me. She grins. Her smile is like a brace factory.

"Yeah. Hi. I'm Violet." She announces it like I should know what that means.

I stare at her hard, trying to remember if we've met. She's wearing black leggings and an oversized Minion T-shirt and she's carrying a small grey bag over her shoulder.

"I just had to see your house," she says. "Can I come in?"

Before I can think of an answer, she's pushing her way past me. By the time I catch up with her, she's already in the kitchen. And she's lifting a professional-looking black camera out of the bag, along with a small notebook and pen.

"Sorry, do I know you?" I ask.

"Nope." She loops a strap around her neck, holds the camera up to her face, and adjusts the lens. "This place is unbelievable."

"Um . . . thanks?" I reply, unsure what else to say to the strange girl in my kitchen. I feel like I should ask her to leave, but I don't know how to do that without hurting her feelings.

Click, click, click.

"So you've really lived here all your life?"

"Yeah," I reply. "Wait, how do you know that?"

She lowers the camera for a second and scribbles something in her notebook. "And is it always this dark? And quiet?"

Click, click, click.

I take two steps toward her, cautiously, like you'd approach a growling dog. "I really don't think my parents would like you taking pictures of our—"

She waves me off with a freckled hand. "Oh, don't worry. I'm not going to post them on my blog or anything. They're just for my personal archives."

"I still don't—"

"You're Daisy, right? I didn't think you'd be so short."

She holds the camera up to my face and snaps a close-up. I freeze. Now this is really getting weird. "How did you—"

Click, click, click.

She peers at me over the top of her lens.

"Oh, I've heard all about you. And your family. Speaking of which, is your brother home? I'd like to meet him too. But I don't have a lot of time. They'll be home soon. Where are the bedrooms, please?"

She muscles her way past me into the living room. I follow close on her heels, slapping my cheeks to try and wake myself up. This *has* to be a dream.

"Listen, I don't know how you know my name or why you're interested in my house, but—"

She stops walking so suddenly, my face slams into her back.

"Ow!" I say, rubbing my stubbed nose.

"Did you really just ask why I'm interested in your house?" She looks annoyed. As if I've said something to offend her.

"Well . . . yeah."

She shakes her head, holds her arm out wide, and wiggles her fingers. Like she's a magician trying to conjure up a spell.

"Would ya look at this place!" she shrieks.

"Hey, keep it down. My dad's sleeping."

But it's like she didn't even hear me 'cause she just keeps shrieking.

"I guess maybe you just can't appreciate it because you live here. But take it from me, if you didn't live here, you'd be plenty interested! This house is a veritable phenomenon! A study in untamed nature! A *National Geographic* feature just waiting to be shot!"

My jaw falls open. "What the *crux* are you talking about?"

Before she can give me an answer, Jack's voice floats down the staircase. "Laze, be quiet. Dad's sleeping."

"Oh, is that your brother?" psycho-girl asks, raising her camera again.

"Jack?" I whisper-yell, inching toward the stairs. "Get down here. Hurry, please!" If there was ever a time I needed my own personal bodyguard, it's right now.

"Goodie," she says, holding the viewfinder up to her face and adjusting the focus.

A second later, Jack comes charging down the stairs — so fast and fluid, he's like a one-kid Niagara Falls.

"I couldn't find a dictionary, but I called Grappa and he looked your words up on his iPad. You're so busted." He freezes when he sees the girl. "Who's this?" he asks, flicking his hair out of his eyes so he can get a better view.

Click, click, click.

"Not sure, but she said she's violent," I explain, pulling him to my side.

"Violet, actually," she says. "Violet Pitt." Putting down her camera, she takes Jack's hand and gives it a vigorous shake. "Nice to meet you." Then she reaches around him and tries to do the same to mine, but I manage to pull my hand away before she can touch it.

Her forehead scrunches up like an accordion. She chews on her bottom lip and stares at me thoughtfully.

"Did I scare you?" she asks, holding up her palms like she's surrendering to the police. "Didn't mean to. Sorry."

I have to take a couple of deep breaths so I can unlock my voice. "Did you say you're a Pitt?" I ask.

"For sure. Me and my brother are staying with our great-aunt and uncle this summer. Our parents are in the middle of a divorce but they think we don't know. They sent us away so they can fight it out all day without us overhearing. We got here on Thursday. I'm your new next-door neighbour."

She says it with such a big metallic smile that for a

flash of a second, I kinda want to like her. But if she's a Pitt, she's the enemy. Case closed.

I glance over at Jack, hoping he'll know what to do. My brother's way better at dealing with strangers than I am. When we were little, he used to walk up to strangers at the park or in the grocery store or at the bus stop and just start conversations about nothing. Of course, they all listened and talked back to him, like it was the most normal thing in the world to chat with a random babbling kid you didn't know. Even as a toddler, he was charming.

"I got this, Daisy," he whispers, taking a step forward. He clears his throat and pulls back his shoulders, puffing out his chest to try to make himself look bigger and, I assume, less adorable.

"Sorry, Violet," he says, dipping his chin and lowering his voice into his chest, "but you have to leave before our dad wakes up. He's a security guard. The real deal with a badge and a walkie-talkie and everything. And if he finds you trespassing in our house, he's going to arrest you."

Of course, that's a total bluff. If Dad was awake, he'd probably offer her a glass of lemonade and invite her to stay for dinner. But Violet doesn't know that.

She stares at us in shock. Her smile is gone. Her face is like a landslide.

"You want me to leave?"

"Affirmative," he replies, most officially.

She looks from Jack to me and back to Jack again. All of a sudden, her freckles go pale. She looks so small and scared, for a second I can't remember why I was so freaked out a minute ago.

"Don't wake your dad. I'm not a trespasser," she says. "I didn't come over to hurt anyone. I swear."

"Then what are you doing here?"

"Investigating."

Jack's eyes narrow. "What do you mean, investigating?" he asks. His fake deep voice is squeaking a bit under the strain.

Violet plops herself down on the footstool. Her camera case lands at her feet. Her face falls into her hands. "I was just so curious," she groans through her fingers. "Auntie Ray and Uncle Karl talk about you guys all the time."

I glance at Jack. "They talk about *us*?"

Violet's head bobs up and down. "And your parents. But especially your house. The vines, the animals, the weeds — they talk about it like it's alive. I just had to see it for myself." She lifts her gaze to meet ours. Her eyes look huge behind her glasses. Of course, that gets me thinking of Willow's puppy face. Despite everything, I feel my resolve softening a bit.

"They leave the house after lunch every day," she continues, pushing her glasses back into place. "As far as I can tell, it's golf or a bridge club or something old like that. They always leave me and Zack alone for a couple of hours. Usually we watch a movie or text friends back home. But today, I decided to sneak over here. I couldn't help myself." A guilty smile tugs at her lips.

Somebody clearly needs to warn this girl. Jack's still trying to keep up the tough-guy act, so I guess it has to be me. "You know," I say, "if they find out you're here, they'll go ballistic."

Violet stands back up. "Oh, you can't tell them." She shakes her head furiously. "They'll kill me. Or ground me, or make me do push-ups or something. Zack and I are forbidden to talk to you. Or be anywhere near you." She leans forward and whispers, "They *really* hate your family. All of you. Even your cat."

"Yeah, we kinda figured," I say in my best thank-you-captain-obvious voice.

Her gaze lowers. She tugs nervously on the hem of her oversized T-shirt. "I, um, borrowed Uncle Karl's binoculars and I've been watching you from my window ever since I got here. Hope you don't mind. I've just never seen anything like your house. I want to keep shooting it. Like, with my camera."

I stare at her in surprise. "You want to be a photographer?"

"Photojournalist, actually. I like writing too."

Writing? And with that word, the last of my resolve finally disappears. I don't even care that she's a Pitt. Stepping out from beside Jack, I give her hand a shake.

"Nice to meet you, Violet," I say with a smile. "Have you ever been to camp?"

Chapter 9

Mom had to pull a double shift at work. When she finally gets home, she's covered in someone's burger. There are mustard, ketchup and pickle stains all over the bottom of her shirt and jeans. There's even a little bit in her hair. Only thing missing is the bun. I can smell her before she walks into the kitchen.

It's almost eleven o'clock and Jack and I are standing at the counter, spoon-warring over the last of the vegan mango sherbet. Except I'm being nice and letting him win most of the battles.

"What happened to you?" he asks, looking up from the carton.

Mom drops her keys onto the pile of newspapers littering the table. She collapses into a chair. "Four loaded burgers, three sides of fries, a Caesar salad, two Cokes and a coffee," she mumbles, slumping down in her seat. Her arms fall to the side and her head slowly rolls back until her chin is saluting the ceiling. It's like watching a human balloon deflate.

"You dropped a tray?"

"All over myself and a family of four. Food and broken glass everywhere. What a disaster!"

Her voice is trembling and for a second I'm worried she's going to cry. Dropping my spoon, I pull up the chair beside her and reach for her hand.

"Sorry, Frieda. That sucks."

There's a coffee stain in the shape of a wobbly Christmas tree running up the sleeve of her favourite white shirt. And her skin is dry and rough. I try to remember if we have any hand lotion in the house.

She gives my hand a tiny squeeze. "I'm fine, Rabbit," she says, without looking up. "Just exhausted. It was one of those days."

Jack comes to join us at the table. He's carrying the near-empty carton. "Want some sherbet?" he asks, waving the last spoonful over her mouth like it's a dose of medicine. I know he's trying his best to make her smile, but it's not working.

Mom sighs and heaves her head back upright. "Thanks, but I think what I need most is a shower and my pillow."

She winces as she stands and doesn't notice Jack's face fall.

But I do.

With a quick kiss to both of our heads, Mom shuffles out the kitchen door. My heart stings as I watch her go. I wish there was something we could do to help her. Mom and Dad always know how to make us feel better when we're sick or sad. Why is it so hard to do the same for them? I stare at the ring of keys nesting in the mess of newspapers.

"Is she going to remember where she left those?"

Jack shrugs as he follows my gaze to the keys. "Maybe we should move them to somewhere easier to spot?" he says, licking the last of the sherbet from the spoon. "What about the front hall table? Or her purse?"

"We could. But will that just confuse her more? I mean, what if she *does* remember and goes looking for them in the newspapers and they're not there?"

I'm trying my best to imagine how a scatterbrain works, but it's hard.

Jack breathes on the bowl of the spoon and hangs it on the end of his nose. "I think no matter what we do, she'll still spend twenty minutes searching for them," he says, catching the spoon just before it falls into his lap. He yawns and stretches his hands up to the ceiling. "Is Violet coming over again tomorrow?"

"Why? Wanna do a camp program with us?" I give his exposed armpit a poke.

Jack snorts and brings his arms down. "No. But you guys better be careful or Dad's going to find out there's a Pitt in the house. He knows when we're doing stuff behind his back. Even when he's sleeping."

"You haven't said anything, have you?"

Violet's been sneaking over to the Jungle for the past few days. We've been doing camp programs and hanging out in my room, but we have to be quiet so Dad won't hear us. I don't think he'd really mind that I'm becoming friends with a Pitt. But if he knew we were lying to her great-aunt and uncle about it, he'd be upset.

Violet has an iPod *and* an iPad. She hasn't said so but I'm guessing her parents must be rich. She's pretty good at Bananagrams too and she's also a gymnastics freak. She's teaching me how to do a headstand and a standing bridge kickover. We've been having fun. But if the evil Pitts knew, I'd probably never see her again. So believe me, the last thing I want is for word to get back to them.

Jack gives me the side eye. "Come on. You know I can keep a secret, Laze."

"Yeah, I know."

Puh-leese. How could I *not* know? I'm pretty sure he's keeping one from me at this very moment. I'm ready to call him on it, but I change my mind. There's the tiniest hint of something sad hiding behind his eyes. The last thing I want is to make it grow any bigger.

"Why don't I ask her to bring her brother, Zack?" I say instead. "That way you'll have someone to shoot hoops with."

"Sure. Whatever." He stands up and reaches over to pat my head, like I'm a poodle. "I'm going to bed."

"'Kay, good night."

I think about the keys for a few minutes after he's gone. I guess one of us could just get up early and show Mom where they are before she leaves for work. But we've been sleeping in every day for the past two weeks. Getting up early won't be easy. Leaving the keys, I walk over to the junk drawer under the banana hanger. I rummage through a sea of coupons, elastic bands and old busted-up toys until I finally find what I'm looking for — an old pack of neon-pink Post-its and a broken brown crayon. I write a bunch of notes for Mom, telling her where to find her keys tomorrow morning. I write as many as I can until I run out of paper, then I post them all over the house in the places she'd be most likely to look. One on the front door, one on the hall mirror, one on the toilet flusher, one on the telephone and one on the handle of the coffee pot. It's like a trail of neon-pink breadcrumbs for her to follow.

Satisfied, I snap off the lights and head upstairs to my room. A muffled noise stops me as I'm passing by Jack's door. I tilt my ear closer so I can hear better. I think he's crying. Not a sobbing-and-wailing-and-I-don't-care-who-hears-it kind of cry, but more of a pitiful-whimpering-softly-into-a-pillow variety.

Oh, Toe.

I reach for the doorknob, but pause with my hand in mid-air. What am I going to say to make him feel better? I know he feels guilty sometimes because, well, sometimes he tells me so. Also, I saw the way he looked at Mom tonight, like maybe this is his fault — the double shifts Mom and Dad have to work, and the vines that took over the windows, and the evil Pitts complaining about us, and me not growing. I think he's decided that if he was never sick, none of these problems would exist (which might technically be true, but it still doesn't mean he should blame himself). That's a whole lot of guilt for a twelve-year-old kid to handle. I hover in front of his door. Maybe I should go in and give him a hug and tell him a silly joke or a corny Dad-quote to make him laugh? And then maybe I could break out into a dramatic rendition of "Let It Go" and convince him that none of this is his fault because this is just the way the universe works.

But maybe if I do, he'll feel grateful and then he'll open up and tell me the truth about what's really going on with that super-secret doctor's appointment last week.

My hand drops down to my side.

Maybe, just maybe, I don't really want to know the truth after all.

Told you I'm not brave.

So, yeah, I chicken out. Sending invisible hugs through the closed door, I scurry up to the safety of my room. The rest of the night is like a galactic wrestling match. I toss and twist under my sheets, worrying about the lines on Mom's forehead, and the stains on her shirt, and the dry skin on her hands, and Jack's life, and Willow's missing letters, and what

I will do when I grow up if I can't be a writer. The wind whistles around my walls, rattling the windows like it's trying to blow them off their frames. If I let it in, where would I want it to take me? Antarctica to see the penguins? Disney World? The Great Wall of China? After a couple of pillow flips, I decide to go to the Dead Sea. I picture myself floating away on soft, warm waves with the sun on my face. It must feel like flying.

The vines sigh and whisper in the wind, like they're trying to lull me to sleep. But it doesn't work. I flip my pillow over, turn onto my side and cuddle my soft, sticking-out belly like it's a security blanket. That doesn't work either. So I pull out my flashlight and start crosswording. I finish the whole *shizzling* book, but I still can't fall asleep.

Sometime around three o'clock, I get up and tiptoe downstairs to Jack's room. He's lying on his side and snoring softly. I lift the blanket, climb into bed beside him, put my head on his pillow and comfort myself with the sound of his breath, like I used to all those nights in the hospital. I want to tell him that he's going to be okay no matter what, that I'm watching out for him, that I love him. But I don't say anything because he's sleeping so peacefully and I don't want to wake him up. Hours pass and eventually I hear the faint sound of the front door opening and closing and I know Dad's getting home from work. By the time the first bit of daylight starts pushing through the leaves covering Jack's window, I haven't slept a wink. But I've done some good thinking.

I have another idea.

When we were six years old, Jack got stuck in the toilet. Truly. He was just sitting there innocently reading a comic book and doing his business. But when he was finished and tried to stand up he couldn't. His skinny little bum was stuck inside the seat. He freaked out and started screaming and Grappa and I came running to help, but he'd locked himself in and couldn't get up to open the door. Grappa was babysitting us, but he didn't know what to do so he picked up the phone to call 911. I guess he figured a firefighter could break down the door with an axe and rescue Jack before he ran out of breathable air in there. Luckily, that didn't have to happen because I managed to pick the lock with a paper clip (I think I must have read about someone doing that in a book once) and pull him free. He was crying and the skin around his bum was pinched and red, but otherwise he was fine. Still, to this day, Jack won't ever close the bathroom door all the way. Not even when he's making a stinker.

Poor kid.

Two summers ago, we went on a road trip to Sandbanks and the very first day there, we lost him. It was during a heat wave and the beach was jam-packed with sweaty bodies looking for a way to cool off. While the rest of our family was chilling and sharing the shade under our beach umbrella, Jack had wandered away without anybody noticing. By the time we figured out he was gone, he'd completely disappeared into the crush of the crowd. My parents panicked. Nobody knew how long he'd been gone. Mom ran one way down the beach while Dad ran the other, both of them screaming Jack's name at the top of their voices, yelling for strangers to help find him and begging anyone who'd listen to call the police and close down the roads. In the end though, Jack wasn't on the beach at all. Half an hour later, I found him floating on his back in knee-deep water, singing "Do You Want to Build a Snowman?" Turns out he'd walked away to look at a sand sculpture and couldn't find his way back to our umbrella. Instead of looking for us, he'd gone into the water to wait. "The sand was hot under my feet," he explained after I brought him back to Mom and Dad.

My point? I've saved my brother's life a bunch of times already. Why not try for one more? I'm not a doctor, but I think I can help.

Picking up my flashlight, I scoot downstairs and head out to the backyard. Flicking on the flashlight, I search through the prickles and the last of the berries until I find that stupid book about the girl who knows how to fix every problem.

If she can do it, why can't I?

Chapter 10

Dear Willow,

Guess what? I met the evil Pitts' grand-kids. Well, actually, their grandniece and nephew. And actually, so far I've just met the girl. Their names are Violet and Zack and they're spending the summer next door. Of course, the evil Pitts made a rule that they're not allowed to talk to us, but that doesn't stop Violet. Every day after lunch she sneaks over for a Junglecamp program. I can't tell Mom and Dad because they wouldn't like us sneaking around. Hope you don't mind, but I made her a junior counsellor. Yesterday we did Archery in the backyard with some rusty fondue forks and Jack's old dartboard. The day before that, we had Music History and we memorized the songs on Taylor Swift's first album. It was great, but not the same without you (obviously). Later today, we're planning on doing Creative Writing. She says all I need is one good idea to get me going. Now I just have to figure out what it is.

Early this morning, I overheard Mom and Dad whispering in the kitchen when they thought I was upstairs sleeping. Apparently Jack's got more doctors' appointments next week. Nobody will give me details, and I'm sure he's getting sick again because they're being all strange and secretive. But I've decided not to freak out about it. Not even a bit. Because I'm coming up with a plan to save him. I'll explain more later but I have to go now because I'm getting close to the end of the page and I have to save my last piece of blank paper for Creative Writing this afternoon.

Hugs and stuff,

Daze

P.S. I'm not totally miserable anymore.

Hope you're not either. Does satisfaction love company?

P.P.S. Yes, the raspberries are ready. I didn't save any for you. Sorry. Are you mad?

P.P.P.S. Write back soon! And make it a real letter this time!

P.P.P.P.S. How's Couchikoo?

Chapter 11

Mom took another day off work because she and Dad have to take Jack to an appointment. It must be the one I overheard them talking about last week. I'm worried it's going to be long because they asked Grappa to come spend the afternoon again. Which is fine with me. I need his help anyway.

He strides through the front door a few minutes before noon, smiling and so cool in his black leather pants and a glittering skull T-shirt. He looks just like that wrinkly old rock star from last century who still tours every summer. I can't remember the guy's name right now, but you know who I mean. Grappa swoops me up and gives me one of his great bear hugs — so squeezy, I can hear our bones crack.

But his smile fades when I tell him I want to take a pass on the zoo.

"What? You want to hang out *here* today? Why?"

The way he says "here" makes it sound like my house is an alligator-infested swamp.

"Sorry, but I have stuff to do. You can help."

"What kind of stuff?"

After swearing him to secrecy, I sit him down at the kitchen table so I can fill him in on my plan to save Jack. Well, actually, just one part of my plan. I don't tell him the rest. Like how I've been smashing up my vitamins and secretly slipping them into Jack's smoothies and homemade muffins for the past week. Or how I've been waking him up early, yanking him out of bed, and forcing him to go jogging with me because I read somewhere that daily exercise is the key to living a long life. Grappa doesn't need *all* the details.

"So, what's this plan of yours?" he demands.

"First, put away your phone," I say. I wait quietly for him to shut down Candy Crush. I want to know that he's really listening.

With a sigh, he pops it into the front pocket of his shirt. "Okay. Spit it out."

"Well, today I thought . . . I thought we could try to open Jack's bedroom window."

He doesn't look impressed. At all.

"Why the heck is that a secret?"

"That's not the secret part. It's just that fresh air's important for your health. And sunshine too. You know, vitamin D and all that stuff? I don't think Jack's getting enough. There're too many vines."

"I see. And Jack gave you his permission to do this?"

I shake my head. "It's going to be a surprise."

He leans back in his chair and studies my face. "Tell me, why exactly do you think you have to save him? Did someone tell you he's getting sick again?"

"Well, not in so many words," I say, crossing my arms and shoving my thumbs into my armpits. "But I'm sure something's going on. Everyone in this house is acting weird. And secretive. Like today, did Frieda even tell you why they're at a doctor's appointment *again*?"

He scratches the back of his head. "She didn't go into detail. But if there was something to be worried about, I'm sure your mother wouldn't keep it from me."

"Maybe, maybe not. Either way, I'm going to get that window open. It can't hurt, can it?"

Grappa shakes his head. "Crazy Daisy," he grumbles. But I can see the glint of a smile in his eyes.

"So, are you in?"

"Fine," he says, pushing on the table and standing up. "What do you need me to do?"

I grab his hand and drag him toward the front door. "Follow me."

Our garage is a junk heap. I don't go in there very much because it's piled with so much stuff, there's barely enough room to scratch an itch. And it smells horrible — like a mixture of oil spills, mouldy newspapers and rotting leaves. Moving quickly, we manage to dig out Dad's rickety old ladder, drag it to the backyard, and prop it up against the vines. Clapping the dust off my hands, I point up to the spot where I think Jack's room must be. "Okay. Now all you have to do is find the right window and start clearing it."

Grappa looks up, shielding his eyes from the glare of the sun. His gaze follows the line of my finger. "You want *me* to climb up there?"

I can tell by the tone of his voice there's a battle coming.

"It's only two storeys."

He drops his hand and turns to look at me. "Why don't *you* do it?"

"Because you're so much bigger than me. And stronger. Those vines are tough."

He doesn't look convinced. "I don't know, Daisy. I'm not as young as I used to be. What makes you think this is a good idea?"

Taking both of his hands in mine, I do my best impersonation of Willow's begging-puppy eyes.

"Please, Grappa? For Jack?"

"For Jack?" he snorts. "What about me? I'm rather fond of my bones, you know."

"Don't worry. I'll hold the ladder. You won't fall."

"How can you be so sure?"

"Because . . . because look at you. You're so strong and fit. You're the youngest seventy-five-year-old I know. How's it even possible that you're a *grandfather*? It'll be a piece of cake for you."

I know it's a risk bringing up his age. We're not supposed to mention it, like ever. But if Grappa has a weakness, it's his vanity. His favourite thing in the world is when people tell him he looks way too young to be a grandfather.

"Fine. But who told you I was seventy-five?" he grumbles, reaching for the ladder. He tugs his silver skull link bracelet off and hands it to me for safekeeping. "I'm really not dressed for this, you know."

"I know," I say, slipping it into my pocket. "But you're awesome. Thanks for helping, Grappa."

He takes a step up, steadies himself for a second, then another step. His black motorcycle boots clunk heavily against the metal rungs. Little by little, he makes his way to the top. I cheer him on from the ground below.

"You got this! Just a bit farther! Looking good!"

As soon as he gets there, he starts ripping away at the vines. I hold the ladder steady while he works. It must be hard because I can hear him swearing a blue streak and grunting from the exertion. After a minute or two, a rustling shower of leaves and thick ropey stalks begins to fall.

Sif, sif, sif they go as they land in a heap beside me. I know it's crazy, but it sounds like the Jungle's laughing at us.

"Do you see the window yet?" I yell up.

"No!" He swats something away from his head. "But I do see wasps!" A few more swats are followed by a rant about my parents and our damned overgrown house. Maybe it would have helped to send him up with a pair of scissors. Or a knife. I feel a twinge of guilt. He's probably really wishing I'd just let him take me to the zoo.

"How about now?" I ask after five more minutes have passed. I'm staring up at where he's working, looking for signs of a window. But it's impossible to see anything from where I'm standing.

"Okay, I think maybe I found it," he calls down, dropping a particularly long vine onto my head. "But man, these things are thick. And sticky. It's going to take a while to clear enough leaves to get the window open."

"Don't worry. We've got lots of time!"

He answers with a grunt.

A second later, I gasp when I feel a hand on my bare shoulder.

"Yo!"

I spin around to find Violet's big metallic grin right in front of my face. I must have been so focused on Grappa and the vines, I didn't even hear her coming up behind me.

"*Schnitzel!* You scared me! I almost peed my pants."

"Sorry," she says, picking a leaf off my sleeve. "I tried knocking on your front door, but you didn't answer. Whatcha doing? And why's that biker dude pulling down your vines?"

"That's my grandfather. And I asked him to. I want to open Jack's window."

"Ah." She nods knowingly. I've already told her about my plan to save him. She's actually the one who came up with the plan for slipping him my vitamins. And it was her idea to search the Jungle for life-saving plant species.

"Did you know that over fifty thousand kinds of plants can be used for medicine?" she explained yesterday, as we waded through the backyard collecting as many different kinds of leaves as we could find. "I'm sure the one to save Jack has to be growing out here somewhere!"

"But if there are fifty thousand to choose from, how are we going to know the right one when we find it?" I asked, circling a patch of prickly weeds.

If she answered that question, I didn't hear her. Because that was the moment she found the poison ivy. Coincidentally, it was also the moment our short search for life-saving plants came to a crashing halt.

Lucky for Violet, the rash was pretty small. We patched it up with some of Mom's aloe vera plant and a roll of gauze and she was okay — although not overly eager to get back to leaf collecting.

"But he's only going to clear one window, right?" she asks, pointing up at Grappa.

"Yeah, don't worry."

Violet's pretty crazy about the vines. Sometimes I wonder if we'd be friends at all if it weren't for the Jungle.

She peers over my head and gestures frantically at something behind me. "I brought Zack like you asked. I thought our brothers could hang out today."

"But Jack's not here." I glance over my shoulder, curious to see her brother. I scan the backyard, but don't see anybody there.

"Bummer. You want to meet him anyway?"

"Sure."

"Get out here, Zack!" Violet hisses. "Come on, she doesn't bite." She tilts her head toward me and rolls her eyes. "Sorry, he's a little shy," she whispers. "I think my aunt and uncle really freaked him out about your house."

"Um. That's okay," I say, straining my eyes for signs of this mystery boy.

A moment later, he steps out from behind the

snowball bush. He's wearing cargo shorts, a black T-shirt and a baseball cap that has "We The North" printed in big letters across the front.

Jack would go nuts over that cap, I think to myself.

"Hi," he says, giving me a mini wave. Pushing his cap back, he shoves his hands in his pockets and starts walking toward us. He's about the same height as his sister. And he's got the same sticking-out ears. But that's where the resemblance ends. Not one freckle. Brown hair instead of red. Perfectly shaped eyebrows. No braces either. And a pair of the deepest dimples I've ever seen.

"Zack, this is Daisy. Daisy, this is Zack."

"'Sup?" I say, letting go of the ladder with one hand and mini-waving him back.

"Hey." His brown eyes shift from me to the Jungle. "Cool vines. Is that your gardener?"

"Thanks. Nope, my grandfather."

"Really?" He smiles like I've just said something funny. For some reason, I find myself smiling too.

"My brother's out," I say. "Sorry. I know you wanted to meet him."

He stops smiling as his gaze snaps back to me. "Oh. I can come back tomorrow if that's better."

"No, don't go. You just got here," Violet says, grabbing his arm. "Maybe you can be a special guest counsellor. That okay, Daisy?"

My jaw drops. For a moment I'm completely speechless. *Special guest counsellor?* She's not allowed to be making up new rules. Did I forget to explain that I'm the director? I try to think of a way to explain this without sounding bossy.

"We *are* still on for camp, aren't we?" she asks. "I got my notebook and my lucky pen. And my camera." She holds up the grey bag as evidence.

"Oh. Yeah. Sure. We can start as soon as Grappa and I finish out here. But—"

"Great. Just remember, we only have an hour before our aunt and uncle get back. Oh, and I brought some writing exercises to get you going. I learned them at a book camp I went to last summer."

Well, this is awkward. I feel my cheeks go warm. "Writing exercises? What, like word yoga?" I mumble, sneaking a glance at Zack.

"Yeah, totally," she giggles. "And some pencil push-ups too." Violet's laugh is so funny. It sounds like a mix of a sneeze and a pig snort.

"So how much longer till you guys are finished out here?" she asks.

I cup my hand around my mouth like a bullhorn. "How much longer you think?" I call up to Grappa.

"Almost done," he yells from above. The ladder wobbles and I tighten my grip to steady it. "Hey, watch it down there," he barks. "You still holding on?"

"Of course."

The rain of leaves suddenly stops. "Who're they?" he yells, pointing at Violet and Zack.

"Just the neighbours' grandniece and nephew."

Violet elbows me in the ribs.

"Ow!"

"You aren't supposed to tell anyone we're here," she hisses.

"Oops. Sorry."

"Your neighbour? You mean the cranky old guy with the suitcase?" Grappa hollers. "Isn't he your sworn enemy?"

"Um, yeah," I reply, trying not to laugh at Grappa calling Mr. Pitt old when they're probably the *exact* same age. I glance sheepishly at Violet. "He asked," I tell her with a shrug. "And I'm not very good at lying."

"I'm coming down now," Grappa says. The ladder

shakes as he starts making his way back to the ground. I focus on keeping it steady so he doesn't crash-land. By the time he steps off the ladder, his grey curls are covered in a crown of stems and leaves, he's panting and thin streams of sweat are running down his tanned face.

"Okay, it's done," he huffs, flicking a pair of ladybugs off his arm. "Hope you're happy." He nods at the Pitts. "Nice to meet you. You say you guys are friends?"

I kick at the pile of vines at my feet. "Yeah, but it's a secret. So don't tell my parents."

Grappa winks. "No worries, kid." He leans down and whispers in my ear. "I see you took old Abe Lincoln's advice after all."

He slips his skull bracelet back on and takes my hand in his. Together we step back from the house to look at what he's done. I gasp as soon as I see it.

"Wow, it's so different," Violet says, pulling out her camera and snapping a pic. She's right. That one naked patch over Jack's window sticks out like a bald baby in a barber shop. I figured maybe pulling the vines off Jack's window would make my house look a little more normal. Instead, it looks weirder than ever. After a minute of staring, the four of us troop inside for a late lunch. Grappa gets a pot of macaroni going while Violet, Zack and I go upstairs to check out Jack's room. Luckily, Grappa's work looks way better from the inside. I happy-clap when I see the sunlight washing Jack's dingy walls in a hazy glow.

Click, click, click. "It looks like a dream," Violet gushes from behind her camera lens. "Or a sparkly unicorn . . . or a Disney Princess movie. Jack's going to love it. It's perfectly *divine*!" She laughs and nudges me with a very pointy elbow. "Get it? *De-vine?*"

Normally, I'd be all over that pun. But right now, I've got more important things on my mind. I march over to the window. As soon as I manage to force it open, fresh air rushes past me with a *whoosh*. I can practically hear the house slurping it up, like it's quenching a long thirst. The fresh air fills every stale corner of the room. I take a deep breath and let it out slowly.

This is going to help Jack, I think to myself. My eyes flood with tears. I hurry to cover my face so Violet and Zack won't see. I don't get it. Why, in the happiest moments, do I feel like all I want to do is cry?

Chapter 12

It's just after five in the afternoon when they get home. Dad leads the way, striding into the kitchen carrying a bag of KFC. I stare at it in surprise. How on earth did he convince Mom to let him buy that?

"Picked up dinner for you and me, Daisy," he says like it's no big deal, setting the grease-stained bag down on the counter. "Where's Grappa?"

"He had to go," I say, unfolding the top and taking a sniff. I have to know if this is the real thing or just a cruel tease. "He has to walk the pig and the dog before his date tonight."

One deep-fried whiff confirms it. I glance back up at Dad. He gives his head a little shake as if to say, *Don't ask too many questions.* What the *crux* is going on? Mom doesn't usually allow this kind of food into the house. The last time KFC passed through the doors of the Jungle was last winter for Dad's fortieth birthday dinner. Did I forget my parents' anniversary? Or is this some kind of a health food rebellion? Or . . . oh no . . . comfort eating?

My eyes bounce over to Jack. He looks okay to me, except for a small Band-Aid on the inside of his elbow. I can't help noticing that today's appointment didn't take nearly as long as the last one. I'm really hoping that's a sign my secret plan's working, but I'm not going to say anything 'cause I don't want to jinx it.

While Dad gets busy unpacking our chicken and fries, Mom and Jack start chopping veggies for a salad. I can't understand how those two health nuts refuse to eat fast food, even when it's sitting right in front of them in all its greasy glory. It's a total mystery to me how anybody can live on granola and quinoa day after day, then resist the smell of fried food when it presents itself.

I grab some plates and hurry to set the table so we can all sit down to eat together. Family dinners in our house happen so rarely on a weeknight, I can't even remember the last time we did this. Mom and Dad look kind of distracted, so I try to keep the conversation chatty by talking about my day. I'm careful, of course, not to say anything about Violet or Zack.

Dad listens to me with a funny look on his face. His eyebrows look pinched and he's scratching his beard a lot.

"So you and Grappa *gardened* this afternoon?" he asks.

"Yeah, just a bit in the backyard. The vines needed some pruning." I don't give away any more details because I really want it to be a surprise for Jack.

Dad glances over at Mom. She just shrugs. He snorts and stuffs a french fry into his mouth. "Your grandfather must have *loved* that."

I can tell Mom's trying not to smile. She clears her throat and stabs some salad onto her fork. "What happened to the zoo plans?"

"I don't know. Just wasn't in the mood."

"You shouldn't go to the zoo anyway," Jack says, taking a gulp of his tomato juice. "Keeping animals in cages is cruel."

"Oh, I don't know about that," Dad says, wiping some stray crumbs out of his beard. "Free food and shelter? Good medical care? No bills to pay? Doesn't sound like such a bad life to me."

"Nathan!" Mom clucks.

Dad stands up and deposits his plate in the sink.

"Sorry, but I gotta run," he says, circling the table and kissing each of our heads. "I can't be late for my shift."

The subject of the vines doesn't come up again that night. Maybe it's because the window's closed or maybe it's because it's dark by the time he goes up to bed, but Jack doesn't notice the extent of Grappa's and my "pruning" until early the next morning. When I wake up to the sound of him calling my name, I jump out of bed and race downstairs to his room.

"You okay?" I gasp, bursting through his door. He's sitting up in bed, facing the window and shielding his eyes from the sun. The golden light streaming through his hair makes it look like he's glowing.

"Is this what you and Grappa did yesterday?" he asks, not taking his eyes off the view for a second.

"S-surprise!" I say nervously. For the life of me, I can't tell if he's happy about it or not.

He kicks off his sheets and hops over to the window. With a grunt, he hauls it open. Fresh air and twittery birdsong fill the room. Jack closes his eyes and smiles.

"So does this mean you like it?"

"No," he says, tilting his face toward the rising sun. "It means I love it."

"Okay, good," I say, letting out the breath I didn't realize I was holding.

"What are you two doing up so early?" Mom asks, coming up behind me. She puts a hand on my shoulder but freezes the instant she notices the window. I turn to watch her reaction. She blinks for a few seconds as she stares into the bright sunlight streaming into the room. "Look at that," she says, glancing at me out of the corner of her eye. "You call this pruning?"

"Uh . . . yeah."

She nods, then brings her hands together in single clap, like she's ready to take on a new task. "Right. Well, it certainly makes it bright in here. I guess now we'll need to get you some curtains, Jack."

"No way!" we say at the exact same time.

Mom looks from me to my brother, her eyes wide with surprise. "Okay. Okay." She holds up her palms in surrender. "I didn't know you felt so strongly about it."

"I . . . I just thought it would be good for Jack. You know, vitamin D's pretty important." I feel my face go red as I say the words. It's the closest I've come to admitting my secret plan to save his life. Mom walks over to where I'm standing. She gazes into my eyes for a few seconds, then pushes some wayward hair behind my ear.

"You're very thoughtful, Rabbit," she whispers, leaning down to kiss my cheek.

"Thanks," I whisper back.

"Why didn't we do this before, Mom?" Jack asks. I glance over at him. He still hasn't moved a millimetre from the window. "It's so . . . organic!"

My insides puff up with pride. I'm happy Jack likes what I've done.

"Well, your dad and I tried when you guys were younger," Mom says. "Several times, actually. But those vines are pretty stubborn." She shakes her head in amazement. "You two are acting like you've spent your childhood chained up in a dungeon! I hope you know that sleep-ins are going to be impossible with all this light. Just sayin'."

I walk over to where Jack's standing. "No biggie. We have to get up early for our morning jogs anyway. Right?" I hold up my knuckles for a fist bump.

"Right. I guess," he says, bumping me gently.

Mom notices the time on Jack's alarm clock. "Whoops. I better get moving." She's already dressed for her shift and I can see the spot on her shirt where she tried and failed to get rid of that Christmas-tree coffee stain from last week. Mom's never been much good at laundry. "Enjoy the light while you can," she adds, "because those things are going to grow back fast. Trust me. Mother Nature is a powerful force." She pats her pockets and glances around the room. "Anyone seen my—"

"Next to the recycling bin," I say.

She blows me a quick kiss. "Thanks!" And then she's gone.

"We better get moving too," I say, nudging my brother away from the window. "Get your running shoes. It's jogging time."

Jack groans as he squats down to dig them out from under his bed. "Remind me again why we're doing this?"

I know jogging's not his favourite thing, but so far he's been going along with it for me. I told him I was taking his advice and trying to make healthier choices and I wanted him there for support. How could he say no to that? Also, I think he wants to make sure the evil Pitts don't turn their garden hose (or anything else for that matter) on me again. Told you, he takes his job as my personal bodyguard seriously.

The first time we went jogging, we only made it around the block once. That was mostly because Jack insisted on leashing up Bobcat and bringing him with us. But the dumb cat wouldn't jog and stopped to rest in every patch of shade. It took us forever! And then he decided to take a nap under Ms. Da Silva's Japanese maple tree and we couldn't move him for over half an hour. So while we waited for Bob to wake up, Jack and I camped out on the grass and babysat little Taylor while Ms. Da Silva ran out to the corner store for a carton of milk so she could make pancakes.

"Thanks, kids," she called over her shoulder as she pedalled down the driveway. "I won't be long!"

But it felt like she was gone for hours because Taylor made us sing "The Wheels on the Bus" twenty-two times. It was the saddest excuse for a jog in the history of the universe. Fortunately, the next day I convinced Jack to leave the cat at home and we made it around the block three times.

Today, I'm aiming for four but Jack gets a blister on his heel halfway through and we have to come home for a Band-Aid. On our way back inside the house, I check the mailbox for a letter from Willow. It's empty. *Fritz!* I slam the lid closed and stomp into the house.

Where are all her letters? Last summer, she would have written to me at least a dozen times by now. Is there a postal strike I haven't heard about? Or maybe the mailman's playing a trick on me? I've seen him chatting and being all friendly with the Pitts, so I wouldn't put anything past him. For a minute I consider writing Willow another letter and making it all in capital letters so she'll see just how *frizzling* upset I am. But that's probably not what the Dalai Lama would do. So instead, I pull out my notebook and try to force myself to come up with the first words of my book.

I stare at the blank page and wait and wait. But nothing comes to me. Yesterday, Violet told me I'll figure out what to write as soon as I stop thinking about it so much. She said it like it was the most logical thing in the world, but I still don't understand how I'm supposed to figure something out by *not* thinking about it.

Yesterday's corny Dad-quote was: "Art is a lie that makes us realize the truth." Pablo Picasso was the genius who came up with that one. If it's true though, that *could* explain why I'm having such a hard time writing. Maybe I need to spend more time practising how to lie better.

After lunch, Violet's back for another visit. She's

brought Zack with her again, which I'm happy about. It means Jack's got someone to hang out with too.

"Hey," I say, ushering them inside.

"Hey." Zack smiles and looks around. I swear, it looks like his dimples are winking at me. I'd think it was adorable, if he weren't a boy.

"This is my brother, Jack," I say, pointing him out. "He's, um, here today. You know, as opposed to yesterday when he wasn't." I close my eyes. *Smooth, Daze.*

Just as I expected, Jack gushes when he spots Zack's "We The North" cap. The two of them get straight into basketballish talk, and a minute later, it's like they're BFFs or something. Looks like Zack has gotten over the shy thing pretty fast.

"We're going out front to shoot hoops," Jack yells. He's rummaging around in the front hall closet. I think he must be looking for his ball, but a minute later his head pops out and it's wearing his old Raptors cap.

"Now you two are the twins," I giggle. "Jack and Zack!"

"Have fun," Violet says, taking my hand and pulling me toward the stairs.

Zack lingers by the front door. "You want to come?" he asks. I'm pretty sure he means both of us, but it's hard to tell because he's looking straight at me.

"Thanks. Um, maybe later," I say. I like basketball, even though I'm not the greatest at it.

"No way," Violet says, giving my arm another tug. "I hate basketball. Anyway, we've got camp stuff to do. Toodle-oo."

So the boys go one way, we go the other. On the way up to the attic, I check out Violet's poison ivy rash then give her a quick rundown of today's program.

"Arts and Crafts, baby! We're making duct tape wallets."

"Great," she says. "But can we do a few minutes of gymnastics to start off? I want to show you my new thing."

Without waiting for an answer, she gets down on the floor and stretches her right leg out in front of her. It's nice and straight, but her left leg is bent awkwardly behind. "I've been practising my splits since yesterday. I need you to tell me if I'm close."

Thump, thump, thump. Even through the thick vines, I can hear the distant pounding of the basketball on the driveway. I wonder if I should go outside and ask them to bounce more quietly so they don't wake up Dad.

"How's this?" she asks.

"Um, not bad. You just have to work on straightening your back leg."

"I know that. But am I close?"

Thump, thump, thump.

"Kind of," I say.

"If you push down on my shoulders, I think I can do it."

"I think maybe you should try stretching it first. Like this."

I get down on the floor beside her and demonstrate a couple of good leg stretches. We do them together in silence.

Thump, thump, thump.

"They don't like us very much either, you know?" she says, fanning some air onto her rash.

I stare at her for a long second. "Who?"

"Auntie Ray and Uncle Karl. They didn't want me and Zack to come stay this summer, but my parents guilted them into taking us because there was nobody else to do it."

"How do you know that?"

"I overheard Mom talking to Dad about it before we left."

"But . . . how could they possibly not like you and Zack? You're family."

Violet shrugs. "They've always been that way. They

never invite us or any of our cousins over to visit. And at our grandparents' big Christmas dinner, when we go to hug them they hang back like they don't want to touch us. They just hate kids. I guess it's a good thing they never had any of their own."

"Yeah, totally," I say, shivering at the thought.

"Seriously, though," Violet continues, "they're not all bad. They dropped me and Zack off to go swimming at the community centre pool last weekend. And they bought us ice cream after, when they came to pick us up. I even saw Auntie Ray smile when Uncle Karl ordered her favourite flavour. I wanted to snap a photo, but it was over too fast."

I shrug. "If you say so." I'm sure Violet means well. But I've got a pretty good imagination. And when I try imagining the evil Pitts as sweet and cuddly, I just can't do it.

Thump, thump, thump.

"Hey, do you know Morse code?" she asks.

"No. Why?"

"If we could de-vine another window, I thought we could send each other flashlight messages at night. I used to do it with my neighbour back home."

"Isn't it hard to learn?"

She shrugs. "Yeah, it was fun though. But I guess you and I could just text each other instead."

"I don't have a cellphone."

"Oh yeah. I forgot."

The thumping's stopped. I stop mid-stretch and crane my ear. Are they finished with their game? Maybe they're taking a break. I wonder what they're talking about. Why do I care? I don't even like Zack. He's a *boy*.

"Okay," Violet says, getting back into her splits position. "Ready to try again."

This time she comes much closer to getting it right. "You're almost there. Just a bit more."

"Push down on my shoulders," she commands. Her face is turning red from the strain of holding the stretch. I crawl over on my knees and do what she asks. To my surprise, it actually works.

"Ow!" she groans. "Is this right? Ow!"

"Yes! You got it!" I cheer, not commenting on how uncomfortable she looks. Her eyes are squeezed shut and the bridge of her nose is crinkled so tight, her freckles look like a smudge.

"Quick. Grab my camera and take a pic."

I release her shoulders and glance around the darkened room, looking for her camera case. "I don't see it!"

"Um, Daisy?"

"I'm looking!"

"Daisy!" she yells.

"Are you sure you brought it?"

"Will you get over here? There's, like, an entire family of ants crawling up my leg!"

I peer at her through the darkness. "Whatever you do, don't kill them."

"Whaddya mean? Oh, help me, now they're in my shirt!"

"Don't move, I'll get them off."

Now she's starting to laugh in that funny pig snort-sneezy way. "Th-th-they're tickling me!"

By the time I get to her, she's laughing so hard, she's starting to wheeze. "Please!" she begs, tears streaming down her cheeks. The laughing must be contagious because now I'm doing it too.

"Hold still," I say, rolling her over so I can find the ants. She clutches her stomach and lies on her side, kicking her feet as I scoop the little ticklers off one by one and set them free under my bed. After that, we both need a minute to catch our breath.

"I'm okay, I'm okay," she finally says, sitting up and wiping the last of the tears away. "That was awesome. Have I told you lately how much I love your house?"

"Yeah."

"You guys are *so* lucky."

I shake off the last of my giggles and stand up. "I guess . . ."

"No really, it's, like, the coolest house on the planet."

"Thanks. But you probably wouldn't think so if you had to live here."

Violet's mouth opens so wide, I can see her tonsils. "Are you kidding me? I'd switch houses with you in a second. It'd be like living in a giant tree house."

I don't know what to say to that. So I just shrug.

"You've obviously never been inside my aunt and uncle's house," she says, stretching her right leg out in front of her. "Because if you had, you'd appreciate what you got over here." She takes a deep breath and waggles her fingers at me. "Okay, go find the camera. I'm going to try the splits again."

Again? I don't mind when counsellors make programming suggestions, but this is too much. It's time for the director to take charge.

I walk over to the dry-erase board hanging beside my bedroom door. "Sorry, Vi," I say, tapping my finger on the one-thirty slot. "But it's time for Arts and Crafts."

"Really?" she says, peering at me through the shadows. "Can't we change things up a bit today?" She smiles and her bushy eyebrows rise up, like they're getting ready to leap off her head.

Or make a duct tape wallet.

Or maybe both.

Suddenly an idea hits me. A very brilliant and ultra-sneaky idea.

"Okay, you win," I say, grabbing the eraser and swiping the activity board clean. "Programming change! We're going on a field trip."

Forgetting the splits, Violet jumps to her feet and starts happy-clapping.

"Oooh . . . where?"

"Your house!"

"Wait. What?" She stops clapping and her freckles fall to the floor. "What the heck are we going to do there?"

I pull the cap off the marker with my teeth and write the answer in the freshly cleaned one-thirty slot. All capitals, so she knows the director means business: INVESTIGATING.

Chapter 13

"I don't know if this is a good idea," Violet says, bouncing on her heels. She glances up and down the sidewalk to make sure nobody's watching.

"It'll be fine," I say, nudging her to hurry up. "I promise, we'll be in and out in a flash. Just have your notepad ready, in case we find anything suspicious."

"Remind me what exactly we're looking for again?"

"Clues. Evidence. You know, anything that might explain why they're always so grumpy."

I can't stop thinking about that quote Grappa told me — about how the best way to destroy your enemy is to make them your friend. Maybe if my family understood the Pitts a bit better, we could put an end to this feud.

"Okay, but I don't know what you think you're going to find," Violet says, pulling the key out of her pocket and fitting it into the lock. "I've been living here all summer and I haven't noticed any clues."

"Yeah, but how closely have you been looking for them?"

She shakes her head like she thinks I'm nuts. Her frizzy ponytail swishes like a feather duster over her freckled shoulders. "Okay, then let's go fast." She turns the key and pushes open the front door. "Before anyone spots us," she adds, dashing inside.

I take a deep breath and follow her into the Pitts' house. Behind me, the heavy metal door swings closed with a bang. Now I'm officially standing on enemy territory. And I'm so nervous, my heart feels like it's going to jump out of my chest.

I take a deep breath to calm myself down. The mixed odour of cabbage and cleaning fluids prickles the inside of my nose. My gaze sweeps over the foyer and my first thought is, *Holy stromboli, this house is so neat! And clean!* From the gleaming white tiled floor, to the perfectly painted walls — it's so *frizzling* spotless, my eyes hurt just looking at it.

Violet moves quickly. Flicking off her shoes, she passes through the foyer into an area with plush off-white carpet. She glances back, motioning for me to follow. But I'm still stuck by the front door, too scared to go any farther. I don't think I've ever been anywhere so clean before. Not even Jack's old hospital room could compare to this. What if I mess something up?

"Come on!" she hisses.

You got this, Daze, I think, swallowing the hard lump of nerves that's sticking in my throat. I kick off my shoes and bend to pick them up. I'll need them with me in case we have to make a quick exit. I tiptoe quickly through the foyer, silently congratulating myself for showering this morning. At least my feet are relatively clean.

"Oh gosh, Dad would be so mad if he knew I was here," I say, catching up with Violet. "He hates sneaky stuff." I'm whispering and trying my best to be quiet and invisible. I know it's crazy, but it feels like talking too loudly might leave a stain on this perfect house.

"Yeah, well then we're even," Violet replies. "Because my aunt and uncle would kill me if they knew I brought you over here."

"Don't be ridiculous — they wouldn't kill you, Vi," I say, rolling my eyes. "That would make way too much of a bloody mess on this pretty white carpet."

She giggles and points to the staircase. "Are we starting up or down?"

"Up. Definitely."

"Fine. But we gotta go super fast." She leads the way up the stairs. I follow close behind, eyes wide, on the lookout for clues. So far, every wall we've passed is painted a smooth light beige. It almost looks like someone's dipped the house in a giant vat of vanilla pudding. When we get to the top, I note that the second floor is just as spotless as the first. Not a crumb, cobweb or dust bunny to be found anywhere. This is probably my first clue as to why Mr. and Mrs. Pitt hate us so much. Clearly, they like tidy things. And there's nothing tidy about the Jungle.

"Here's my room," Violet says, pushing open the first door on the left.

I stick my head in and do a quick scan of the space. Single bed, wooden dresser and chair, more vanilla-pudding walls.

"Whoa. Clean much?" I turn to look at her in surprise. I never imagined Violet as a neat freak.

She snorts. "Trust me, I didn't do it. It's all my aunt. She makes my bed in the morning before I'm even out of it. Zack's too."

"Really?" I ask, glancing back at the bed with its neatly tucked corners and perfectly placed pillows. "That's pretty nuts. And possibly a very important clue."

"'Kay, I'll write that down," Violet says, opening her notebook and flipping to a blank page. "Zack's room is across the hall. Do you want to snoop in there too?"

I'm about to say yes, but stop myself before the word passes my lips. What if he left something really personal lying around? Like his underwear? Or his pyjamas? Or maybe a stuffed animal he cuddles for sleeping? That would be way too mortifying. My cheeks go warm just thinking about it.

"No, that's fine," I say, taking a step back. "We can skip it. Anyway, I think if we're going to find a big clue, it would be in your aunt and uncle's room."

"Okay, that's down this way," Violet says, pointing to a set of double doors at the end of the hall. "But let's be fast. I don't know how much time we have before they get back."

We tiptoe down the hall to the master bedroom, careful not to leave any deep, incriminating footprints in the plush carpet. On the way, we pass a large window looking out over the front of the house.

"Duck," Violet hisses, tugging on my shirt. I do, but not before I spot the vines from the Jungle, fluttering in the afternoon breeze. And a quick glimpse of Jack and Zack, still playing basketball in the driveway and totally oblivious to the fact that we're over here on a fact-finding mission. I giggle to myself, imagining how my brother would freak out if he knew.

"Here's their bedroom," Violet says, pushing open the double doors. "Just don't touch anything, okay? They don't even let me or Zack in here."

She stands to the side to let me through. But I freeze in the doorway, too nervous to go any farther. My stomach turns a queasy somersault. This suddenly feels wrong. Really wrong. Like stepping into this room means crossing the line between snooping and spying. As curious as I am to figure out what makes the evil Pitts so evil, I just can't bring myself to do it. Instead, I poke my head slightly into the room and glance around quickly, scanning the space for anything important. But I don't see any clues here. It just looks exactly like a larger version of Violet's bedroom.

"I still don't know what you think you're going to find," Violet says, pulling her phone out of her shorts pocket to check the time. Her eyes widen as a look of panic flashes across her face. "Shoot, it's later than I thought," she yelps. "We better go!" She grabs my elbow and yanks me away from the doorway. "They're going to be home any second."

"Wait! We're not done investigating yet."

But she's already dragging me back down the stairs. "Too bad. We're out of time."

"Please, Vi? I'm almost done. Just another minute so I can look around the main floor?"

She sighs as she peels a vanilla curtain back and peeks out the front window. "We're toast if they catch us, you know?"

"They won't catch us. Promise. You keep watch while I finish up the investigation. If you see them coming, just give the signal and I'll scram out the back door."

"What are you talking about? What signal?"

"I don't know," I say, tiptoeing quickly toward the kitchen. "Clap your hands or whistle or something."

As it turns out, the whole main floor is just more of the same obsessive neatness. From the kitchen to the dining room to the powder room, everything is so perfectly tidy, it looks like it could be straight out of a magazine — if the magazine was the kind to feature outdated furniture and lifeless decor. The last room to check is the living room, which looks out onto the Pitts' perfectly manicured backyard. In the centre of the room, a pair of puffy beige couches face each other like giant sumo wrestlers. There's a marble fireplace that looks like it's never been lit, topped with a wooden mantelpiece showcasing a tidy arrangement of photo frames. Matching wooden bookshelves line the walls. I tiptoe over to read the titles, sensing that I'm on the verge of finding a really good clue. It takes a couple of seconds for me to realize that all the books have been alphabetized. I take a step back.

Crux. This place really takes neat-freakiness to a whole other level.

And that's when I realized what a stupid idea this whole investigation probably was. If there were any real clues to be found, the Pitts likely cleaned them up a long time ago.

Violet was right all along.

A high-pitched whistle pierces the air. I spin around in the direction of the front window. "I see them! I see them!" she hisses, jumping up and down and flapping her arms like a panicked chicken. "They're across the street! Shoot, I knew this was a bad idea."

"Okay, don't worry. I'm out of here," I whisper, making a beeline for the back door. But just as I'm reaching for the handle, I glance over my shoulder to make sure I didn't leave anything behind. That's when my eye catches it — the one thing in this entire house that's out of place. Over on the fireplace mantel, tucked away behind the neat collection of sunset shots and rose bush photos — one small silver frame is facing the wrong way.

That's it.

Suddenly, the patio door slides open and Zack comes bounding in from the backyard, so fast and furious he almost knocks us both over. "Sorry, sorry," he says, grabbing my shoulders to steady us. "You okay?" His eyes widen in surprise when he realizes it's me. "What are you doing?" he hisses. "My aunt and uncle are on their way home."

"They're coming up the driveway!" Violet yelps from the front window. "Get out, Daisy! Quick!"

But I can't run yet. Curiosity has taken control of my senses. Still clutching my shoes with one hand, I race to the mantel, grab the rogue frame, and flip it over. It's an old faded photo of the Pitts. They're dressed in funny styled clothes like Grappa used to wear in the olden days. And they're so young, I barely recognize them. The only reason I know it's them is because they're standing in front of this house and Mr. Pitt's electric-blue classic car is in the driveway. Mrs. Pitt is holding a tiny baby. I can't tell if it's a boy or a girl, but it's wearing knitted booties and a matching hat and it's fast asleep in her arms. Mr. Pitt has a protective arm around her shoulders and the two of them are smiling so wide, I can count most of their teeth.

"Look! I think it's another clue—"

But before I can say anything more, I hear the clicking sound of a key turning in a lock. The picture frame is yanked out of my grip. Now Zack is grabbing my hand. My bare feet slide over the carpet as he drags me away from the mantel. Next thing I know, we're at the back patio door and he's pushing me outside.

"Run!" he says, pulling the vanilla curtains closed behind me.

This time, I do as I'm told.

Chapter 14

It rained again last night. Well, technically it was this morning. I was in bed sleeping when I heard the first drops hitting the roof — which reminded me about the leak over my bed, so I picked up my pillow and switched my head to the other end. Just in time, because a second later the sky threw down. Thunder, lightning and sheets of rain, all topped off with a howling wind that whipped frantically around my attic walls, like I was Dorothy and it wanted to airlift me away to Oz. I tried my best to ignore the storm and go back to sleep, but after a few minutes water started dripping onto my ear and I realized there must be a new leak in my ceiling.

For a minute, I considered bunking with Jack. But Bobcat always hides in my brother's bed during thunderstorms and I wasn't looking for a fight. So I kicked off the covers, ran downstairs to the front hall closet, and dug out my old Hannah Montana umbrella. I climbed back into bed, propped it against my shoulders, and used it as a miniature tent.

Because, of course, an old Hannah Montana umbrella has to have a double identity.

But it didn't end up being as cozy as it sounds. It took me forever to fall back asleep. I kept wondering about that photo on the Pitts' mantel, and why it had been turned backwards. And why they were holding a baby. I pulled the covers up over my head, held my breath, and squinted my eyes. And just-like-that, the whole story was right there in my head. Picture this: Maybe the Pitts really did want to have kids when they were young and they bought that house with all the extra bedrooms and that big blue car 'cause they were planning on raising a family. But what if they couldn't have any kids of their own? So they adopted a baby girl, right? But then what if the birth parents changed their minds about the adoption, showed up, and demanded their baby back? And what if there was a whole long, drawn-out court battle, which the Pitts ended up losing? And after that, they got angry and bitter. And being around kids just reminded them of what they lost.

Yeah, I could see it happening just like that. Couldn't you? It would explain everything.

And then I started worrying that my overactive imagination was going to keep me from falling asleep . . . like, ever again. And then a monstrous clap of thunder shook the house, and I started worrying that the storm was the universe giving me bad karma for snooping. And that it was some kind of sign, and that today was going to be horrible.

Turns out I'm right. But just about that last part.

For starters, I sleep in and miss the morning jog.

"Why didn't you wake me up?" I demand, bursting into Jack's room. He's sitting up in bed, flipping through a comic book. Bobcat's lying across his lap, purring up a lung as he bathes in a patch of sunlight streaming through the window. The air smells fresh and wormy from last night's storm.

"I don't want to jog anymore," my brother says, glancing up from his page.

"What? Why?"

He stretches his arms up and lets out a lazy yawn. "Because I like sleeping in. And because I've decided that getting the extra rest is more important to my overall health than running around the neighbourhood, breathing in exhaust fumes and exposing my unprotected skin to dangerous UV rays." He runs his hand down Bob's fur, from his ears all the way to the tip of his tail. "Plus, I like opening my window and listening to the birds in the morning. It's relaxing. Bob likes it too."

My mouth drops open. I can't believe he's saying this. What about my plan to save his life? "But . . . but . . ." I rake my fingers through my hair, trying to figure out a way to make him change his mind. "What if *I* want to keep jogging? You're just going to let me go *alone*?"

He waves his hand in the air, like he's shooing away a fly. "You'll be fine. The Pitts are never around that early anyway."

"Boo!" I'm so upset, I don't know what else to say. I slam the door behind me and head downstairs, praying there's a box of seriously junky cereal waiting for me in one of Dad's hiding spots.

"Good morning!"

"Ah!" I shriek, clutching my chest. There's Dad, oh-so-calmly sitting at the breakfast table, sipping on a cup of tea and reading the morning newspaper. Like he didn't just scare the socks off me. "What are you doing here?" I gasp. "Why aren't you sleeping? Weren't you working last night?"

“Yes, but I was waiting up to see you.” He puts down the newspaper and pats the empty seat beside him. “Can we talk for a minute?”

Why do I suddenly have the feeling this day is about to get worse?

“Um . . . sure,” I say, walking slowly over to the chair.

Dad smiles. I scan his eyes for that little golden spark of light. But it’s too dark in here to see much of anything.

“You never asked how Jack’s last appointment went,” he says.

“I didn’t?”

He shakes his head.

“Okay. So?” *Where’s he going with this?*

His left eyebrow shoots up. “Aren’t you curious?”

“Not really,” I say, adding a shrug to make the fib look better.

“Is that so?” His head tilts to the side, like I’m a Picasso painting and he’s trying to figure out which angle makes the most sense. I squirm in my seat. “Why not?” he asks.

“No reason,” I say, lowering my head and pretending to pick at a hangnail. *Because I can’t handle hearing that Jack’s getting sick again, and if you say the words it’s going to make it official so I'd just rather not talk about it. Ever. Again.*

"Huh," he says. I can feel his eyes drilling into my face. "That doesn't sound like you. You're normally too curious for your own good."

My knees are suddenly itchy. I scratch at them with the bitten stubs of my fingernails, but it doesn't help. I glance up. Dad's arms are folded in front of him. His eyes narrow.

"Of all the windows in the house, why'd you and Grappa clear Jack's?"

I shake my head.

"Sure there's not something you want to tell me?"

I shake my head again, harder this time. "No. Wait, I mean, yes. There's a leak in my ceiling. Actually, two leaks now. Can we get them fixed before it rains again?"

Dad smiles and for one sweet second I actually think I'm off the hook. "Sure," he says, taking my hand and giving it a squeeze. "But first, why don't you tell me where the fancy camera came from?"

"Wh-what camera?"

"This one." He reaches down and picks up a familiar-looking grey camera bag. "I found it in the living room."

My stomach drops through the floor. *Narf.* Violet must have left her camera here by accident.

"Um . . ." I say, turning my eyes to the wall. To the oven clock. To the bowl of suspiciously brown avocados on the counter. Anywhere but Dad's face. Anything to avoid eye contact.

"Daisy?"

My mind's spinning in circles. *I'm caught! Do I admit my plan to save Jack? Or do I confess about Violet's secret visits? Or how I went snooping for clues in the evil Pitts' house while they were out playing bridge? Maybe all of it? No, that's too much.* I drop my eyes to my hands. Tiny dots of sweat glitter on my palms. I knew I should never have tried to keep a secret from Dad. Let alone three.

"I . . . It's just . . . um . . . nothing, really."

Told you I'm horrible at this. My pitiful attempt at a lie lingers in the air between us like a bad smell. Dad doesn't say anything more. When I finally get the guts to look up, he's staring at me with a start-talking-missy look on his face.

My shoulders droop in defeat. I open my mouth to explain and the truth comes spewing out.

Well, one part of the truth anyway.

"Fine. Violet Pitt's been coming over every day while you're asleep and sometimes her brother, Zack, comes too, but they're not allowed to be here because their evil great-aunt and uncle have banned them from talking to us, so they have to sneak out during their daily bridge game. And even though Violet's a Pitt, she's funny and smart and we have a good time together and she wants to be a photojournalist. And . . . that's her camera case. She must have forgotten it."

Dad's looking at me like I've just lost my mind. "Did you say this girl's last name is *Pitt*? As in, our next-door neighbours?"

"Yeah."

"The same neighbours who've been filing complaints about our home all these years?"

I hang my head. "Yeah."

A bloated silence balloons around us. He really doesn't look happy. His lips are pressed into a tight pink line and he's holding on to his forehead like it's about to fly away. He sighs heavily. "What do you want me to say, Daisy?"

"I . . . I want you to say it's okay. And that Violet and Zack can keep coming over."

He shakes his head slowly. "Honey, I know you

don't like Mr. and Mrs. Pitt. But it's still wrong to be sneaking around behind their backs. Remember what Ben Franklin said about honesty—"

I hold my hands up. "Not now, Dad. Please."

"Fine." He brings his hand to the table with a *thump,* like a judge throwing down a gavel. "But you'll have to tell Violet and Zack that they can't come over anymore without permission. I'm sorry."

I stare at him in shock. "Come on, Dad. Can't you put yourself in their shoes? Would *you* want to be trapped in a house with those two grumps all day?"

"No. But I'm also not looking to start a war with those people. They dislike us enough already."

"Correction: they *hate* us. Violet even said so."

"Which is all the more reason not to make it worse by going behind their backs." He stands up. "I've made up my mind, Daisy. Don't try to change it."

Slumping down in my seat, I stick out my bottom lip and pout. I know I probably look like a bratty five-year-old, but I don't care. "Fine! I'll tell her when she comes over this afternoon. You've just made four kids epically miserable, are you happy?"

"No. But I love you," he says, bending down to kiss my cheek. "Now I'm going to bed."

Without another word, he puts his teacup in the dishwasher and leaves.

Well, that's it, I think to myself. *This day can't possibly get any worse.*

My stomach growls angrily, so I get up and start searching for something to eat. I look through every single cupboard and drawer. I check inside the fridge and on top of it too. I even venture down again to the pantry in our horror-movie-set-of-a-basement — all in search of something good to eat. But there's nothing. Not one box of anything remotely sugary in this whole *shizzling* house!

"How about a smoothie?" Jack says, pouring a scoop of crushed ice into the blender. "I'm making blueberry-kale-spinach this morning."

"No, thanks," I huff. I happen to know he puts raw eggs from his pet chickens in those smoothies. Anyway, by now I'm too grumpy to eat so I go outside and kick at one of the big thorny weeds that have taken over our front lawn. I kick it again and again, until eventually it stops springing back up.

The Dalai Lama doesn't really expect me to be kind to weeds, does he?

Okay, maybe he does. Because once it's flattened, I

feel even worse than I did before. And then I remember what Violet told me about plants saving people's lives. And now I feel gross, like something you scrape off the bottom of your shoe. Squatting down, I grab a twig and try to prop the weed up. But it just flops back over again.

"Sorry, little guy," I whisper, fully aware how ridiculous I must look talking to a weed.

Swallowing my guilt, I stand and slap the dirt off my hands. When I look up, there's Mrs. Smythe, holding her Maltipoo and collecting her newspaper from the end of her driveway. She waves as she bends to pick it up, but her eyebrows look pinched with concern. I know she must have witnessed my fit of weed rage. Is it possible to actually die from embarrassment? She takes a couple of steps in my direction, like she's thinking about coming over for a chat. I decide I don't want to hang around to find out.

"Have a great day, Mrs. Smythe," I call out with a wave. Ducking my head, I rush back to the cover of the Jungle. On my way in, I check the mailbox quickly. A letter from Willow could turn this whole day around. My heart does a little dance when I see something with the Couchikoo logo. Except it turns out to be just another *wizzly* postcard. And this one's shorter than ever.

Hi D,

Camp's great. Hope Jack's okay! See you soon :)

W

What the *crux* is this?

I crumple it into a stiff ball, stuff it in my pocket, and stomp back into the house. Jack's blender is whirring so loudly, I don't even hear Bobcat hissing until I'm almost on top of him. He meows a sharp warning and glares at me.

"What are you looking at, fur-face?"

He stands up, as elegant as a prince, circles me with his nose in the air, then turns and sprints up the stairs. The blender finally stops whirring and I hear Bob's little paws padding down the hall. He must be heading to Jack's room. I follow him there to see what he's up to. My brother and I aren't the only ones who've been enjoying the open window. Ever since Grappa and I de-vined it, Bobcat's been obsessed. The past couple of afternoons, he's spent hours up there on the window ledge, staring out into the backyard.

Sure enough, when I walk in now, he's back in the

same spot. Like Mom predicted, a few vines have already started to creep back over the screen, but for the most part the view is still clear. Bob gazes out, his long black tail hanging down, swishing back and forth like a metronome. Don't know for sure what he's looking for, but I have a few guesses. And they all love to pee on our house.

"Hey, Bob, I got you a ball."

He turns at the sound of my voice and I toss him Willow's crumpled postcard. He bats it away with his paw and sends it skittering under Jack's desk.

"Good cat."

I flop face-first onto Jack's bed, wondering how I'm going to break Dad's decision to Violet and Zack when they come over this afternoon. I mean, how do you *kindly* tell new friends that they're not welcome in your home anymore? I'd like to see the DL try to figure this one out. And what about our investigation? How are we going to finish it now?

The doorbell rings. Once, twice, three times. By the time I make it downstairs, Jack's swinging the door open. The Pitt kids are on the porch. My first thought is: *Why did they come so early? It's not time for camp.* Zack's staring intensely at his shoes. Violet's eyes are red and puffy. It looks like she's crying. My second thought is: *Shazbot.*

Before I can ask what's wrong, she rushes inside and grabs me by the elbows. "We overheard Uncle Karl on the phone with one of the neighbours. We came right over to warn you!" She's talking so fast, I can barely make out what she's saying.

"Calm down. Take a breath."

"I can't calm down," she says, turning away and covering her face with her hands. Only the tip of her freckled nose is showing. "It's just so awful!"

Zack walks up and puts an arm around Violet's shuddering shoulders. He looks worried, but thankfully more composed than his sister.

"What happened?" I ask.

His gaze jumps from me to Jack, then back to me. "Our aunt and uncle . . . It looks like they're filing a complaint to the city about your house."

Oh, is that all? I breathe a sigh of relief. "Don't worry about it," I say, rolling my eyes. "They've filed a ton of complaints before but nothing ever happens. We're not breaking any laws. Right, Jack?"

"Yeah, right," he says. He's laughing because after all these years, the evil Pitts' annual complaints about the Jungle are like a bad joke in our family.

But Zack isn't laughing or smiling. Not even a bit. Not a hint of dimples in sight.

"Well, it sounds like maybe they're trying something new this time," he says. "We heard them talking about petitioning to have the bylaws changed. They've been collecting signatures from every house on the street and apparently they only have a few left to get. It sounded really official. They've even got a date scheduled at city hall to get it approved."

Before I can begin to process what that means, Violet throws her arms around me. I cough a bit as she squeezes the air out of my lungs. "I'm so sorry," she whimpers in my ear. "I can't believe they're doing this!"

I turn to Jack for reassurance. But he looks frozen, like he's been superglued to that one spot. And his perma-smile has all but disappeared.

"City hall?" he says. "When?" There's a hint of fear edging his words.

Zack pulls off his "We The North" cap and holds it over his heart — like this is a funeral and he's paying his last respects to the soon-to-be dearly departed.

"Tomorrow."

Chapter 15

Whoa.

Who'd have guessed the evil Pitts were working on a secret plan of their own this whole time? Turns out that while Violet and Zack thought their great-aunt and uncle were out playing bridge, they were actually hiking up and down Bond Street, knocking on doors, passing out pamphlets, collecting signatures and hatching a sinister plot to bring down the Jungle.

"Do you totally hate us now?" Violet asks, mopping her tear-stained cheeks with the hem of her T-shirt. "I wouldn't blame you if you did."

"Of course we don't hate you." I force myself to smile when really it's the last thing in the world I feel like doing. But I don't want her to cry anymore. "It's not your fault they're out to get us."

She sniffles and hugs me again. Zack shoots

me an apologetic look. "What if Violet and I tried talking to them?"

I shake my head. I'm trying to stay brave, but I can feel my fake smile starting to crumble. "Thanks, but I think that might just make things worse."

"So what else can we do?" he asks. "Do you want us to start a counter-petition?"

"I . . . I don't know," I say, clutching my forehead.

Jack can sense how upset I am because now he's desperately trying to change the subject by inviting the twins to come to the kitchen for a smoothie. Of course. Because even in the face of disaster, he's charming.

"Sorry, we can't," Zack says, prying Violet off me. "Our aunt and uncle could be back any minute. It sounds like the phone call we overheard was from one of the neighbours. I think they ran out to collect his signature before he could change his mind."

"Wait," Violet says, breaking loose and darting back to my side. "I called my mom and asked her about that old photo you found yesterday. Just in case it was a clue like you thought."

"And?" I close my eyes, bracing myself to hear the tragic story — the failed adoption, the bitter court battle, their broken, childless hearts slowly turning to stone.

Violet shrugs. "And nothing. She didn't know anything about it."

My eyelids pop open. "What? Are you sure?"

"Yup. Sorry."

I stare at her in surprise. "But that doesn't make any sense. Why would they keep that photo in a frame? Facing the wrong way in their perfectly organized house? It has to mean something. Unless . . . Oh, unless maybe they didn't tell anyone?"

"What are you talking about? Didn't tell anyone—"

"Shoot!" Zack yelps, swallowing up the rest of her words. "They're coming!" He grabs Violet's hand and steers her toward the door. "We gotta go!"

I run and grab the grey camera bag off the kitchen table. "Oh, hey — you forgot this yesterday," I say, handing it to her.

"Thanks. See you later," she calls over her shoulder.

"Wait—"

But the next thing I know, the two of them are disappearing into the bright morning light. The door closes behind them with a snap. And yup, I totally forgot to mention how they're not allowed to come over anymore. I'll tell them next time. Right now I'm too busy freaking out.

A petition? Changing the bylaws? City hall?

And just an hour ago I thought this day couldn't get any worse.

I stumble to the living room and sink into the couch. My hands are trembling so I sit on them to keep them still. Jack sits next to me, silent as a stone.

"Can they really get away with this?" I ask, leaning my head on his shoulder.

He takes a deep, shaky breath. "I don't know. But let's not freak out, okay? We'll talk to Mom and Dad. They'll know what to do."

"Are . . . are they going to take our house away?" My voice breaks over the question. I have to bite down on my lip to stop myself from crying.

"No. I think the most they can do is make us cut down the vines."

I try to picture the Jungle without the vines, but I can't. As much as I've been secretly wishing for a normal, everyday house, I can't imagine it. Even that old photo I found — back from the year Mom and Dad first moved in — feels like it must have been someone else's home. I think about how much I'd miss my treehouse bedroom. And the sound of the leaves shushing me to sleep every night. And the birds singing in the vines every morning.

But then I think about how much Jack's enjoying the light from his de-vined window. And how sweet the fresh air smells blowing through his room. And how, if our house were normal like everyone else's, kids at school would stop calling me "Weed." A pang of guilt creeps over my conscience. I lift my head and steal a glance at my brother's face. Is there any chance he's thinking what I'm thinking — that cutting down some of the vines might not be such a terrible thing?

"Jack, I—"

The sound of yelling hushes me. It's coming from outside. I turn my ear to the front door. Now a different voice is yelling. It's hard to be sure, but it sounds like it's coming from the driveway.

Jack and I bolt from the couch like a pair of runners leaping out of our starting blocks. The first thing I see when we get outside is Mrs. Pitt. She's standing in front of her prized rose bush. She's wearing her ginormous straw hat and a turquoise track suit that looks like it's the same material as our bath towels.

Her face has gone bright tomato red, as if she's got a horrible sunburn. But I guess it's not a sunburn because she looks so mad, it's like her head is about to explode. One bony hand punches her hip, while the other wags a red-manicured finger in front of Violet's and Zack's faces.

"What did we tell you? How could you go behind our backs like this? We gave you clear instructions to stay away from that house!"

Schnitzel. She must have caught them coming out our front door.

Mr. Pitt's there too. He's clutching a large brown envelope so hard, his knuckles have gone white.

Are the signatures in there?

"But, Auntie Ray, they're not hurting anyone," Violet replies. "Why can't you leave them alone?"

Zack's face has gone pale as a sheet. He raises his hands, palms up — like he's surrendering to a SWAT team. I can hear him talking, but I can't make out the words. That's when Mrs. Pitt spots me and Jack. And all *shikaka* breaks loose.

"Young lady!" she snaps, hopping over her roses and marching up our driveway. "Isn't it bad enough that we've had to endure this mess of a house all these years? And that you've devalued every home on this street? Now you have to go corrupting my niece and nephew?" The red fingernail is wagging in front of my face now. "Stay away from Violet and Zack. Those kids are going through enough this summer."

I'm so stunned, I can't even speak.

"We're not corrupting anybody," Jack says, taking my arm and pulling me to his side. He's trying to sound brave, but I can tell by the quaver in his voice that he's scared too. We're not used to being yelled at. *Is it even legal for grown-ups to yell at kids who aren't theirs?* Out of the corner of my eye, I see Violet hop over the roses and come charging up the driveway.

"Auntie Ray, stop! Please!"

Zack's right on her heels. He takes Mrs. Pitt's hand and tries to lead her away. "Let's go home," he says. But she doesn't budge.

"No. I'm at my wit's end," she huffs, and her cabbage-smelly breath blows in my face and makes me cough. "We've been trying to reason with this family for years. But the parents refuse to think of anyone but themselves."

"That's not true," I say. "Our parents aren't like that."

"Oh, really?" She waves her hands in the direction of the Jungle. "Just look at that house. It's an embarrassment. Why can't your family just be normal like the rest of us?"

I'm suddenly feeling hot all over, like my skin has been lit on fire. There's a bubble of angry words building in my throat. I'm trying so hard to swallow them down, to think kind thoughts and channel my inner DL But I don't know how much longer I can do it. I feel like I'm a balloon that's about to pop.

Mr. Pitt walks over and takes his wife's other hand. "Come on, Ray."

Mrs. Pitt's still watching me. Her blue eyes are like cold steel. "Fine," she says, straightening back up. I breathe a sigh of relief as she starts to walk away. But she's barely taken a step before she turns her head back and spits on the pavement right in front of my feet.

I hear somebody gasp. Maybe it's me. And just like that, something snaps inside me. I can actually feel it happen. Like a tiny pane of glass has been shattered deep in my gut. My hands curl into fists at my side. I pull in a deep breath, stick my chin out, and let loose all the words I've been trying so desperately to hold in.

"You know what? My parents work really hard and they're trying their best and I'm sorry if that's not good enough for you. So *what* if they don't have time for gardening? That doesn't make them bad people!"

I'm yelling so loudly, my throat hurts. But now that I've started, I can't stop. I hold up my finger and waggle it in front of *her* face so she'll know what it feels like.

"My parents are smart and kind and caring. And so's my brother. He's only twelve and he already has the biggest heart in the world. But you? I feel sorry for you because you're just an angry old lady who hates kids and who has nothing better to do than criticize people and go around making stupid petitions."

I pause for a breath. Gentle arms come around my shoulders, but I can't see who they belong to because my vision's gone blurry with tears. I blink hard, trying to make them go away. The last thing I want to do is give the evil Pitts the satisfaction of seeing me cry. But more are coming and I can't stop them so I turn my face as the hot tears spill over my cheeks. I take another breath, and then another. And suddenly I don't feel like yelling anymore. My heart's pounding a wild drumbeat in my ears and my throat feels like it's been scraped raw. The mystery arms squeeze a little tighter, as if they're trying to hold me up. I wipe my eyes and glance around to see who they belong to. Jack, Violet and Zack are all huddled around me like a human shield.

And then I notice the Pitts. They're standing together on the driveway and Mr. Pitt has a protective arm around his wife's shoulders. My thoughts immediately fly back to that old photo with the tiny, sleeping baby. It's almost an exact copy of that scene, down to the electric-blue car in the background. Except there's no baby now. And neither of them is smiling. In fact, Mrs. Pitt's eyes are glassy and it looks like a mini earthquake is taking place on her red lips.

Is she crying too?

She turns and wipes her eyes on her husband's shirt. "How could she say that?" I hear her mumble. "You know that's not true."

"Happy now?" Mr. Pitt says to me. He's not yelling, but there's an angry rumble building in his voice. Like he's a live grenade about to go off. "I've heard enough. Come on kids, we're leaving." He takes Violet and Zack by their elbows and tries to lead them away from our huddle. In the process, his brown envelope falls to the ground, right on top of the small puddle of spit.

After that, everything happens in a blur.

Zack twists around and pulls his arm free, losing his balance and falling butt-first onto the pavement. Violet tries to pull free too, but she's not quite strong enough. "No, I want to stay with Daisy," she says, reaching her hand out to me. I lunge forward and take it, holding on tight and digging my heels into the crumbling asphalt like a one-girl anchor. Mrs. Pitt takes our clasped hands and tries to separate them. That sends Jack into full-out bodyguard mode.

"Don't you touch my sister!" he says, working to untangle Mrs. Pitt's fingers from mine. We're like a human tug-of-war: Team Kid versus Team Evil, with poor Violet as the rope. And nobody's letting go. In the midst of the battle, Zack spots the brown envelope lying on the ground, crawls over, and seizes it. He jumps to his feet, raises his arm over his head, and waves the envelope in the air. The dark spitty circle in the middle looks like a bull's eye on a dartboard.

"Stop it, Uncle Karl! Stop it right now, or . . . or I'll tear this petition to pieces." He brings his other hand up over the top of the envelope, as if he's about to start ripping.

That does it. Mr. Pitt's eyes go wide as golf balls. He drops Violet's arm and lunges forward, trying to grab his precious envelope back. My brother, who can't even bear to see a tiny ant hurt, rushes to the defence of his new friend.

What happens next is an accident.

Probably.

But it happens too fast to be sure.

Chapter 16

Jack's back in the hospital.

Somehow during the tussle over the envelope, he got knocked down and hit his head on the pavement. I know he must have hit it really hard because the sound of it was horrible, like a watermelon being dropped. As I saw him go down, a flash of white light flooded my vision. When it cleared a moment later, all I could see was my twin lying there on the driveway, pale as a ghost and so horribly still. And I felt like all the blood was draining out of my body. I wanted to run to his side. I wanted to scream for help. But I couldn't manage to do either. For a horribly long moment, it felt like I was the one who was out cold.

Finally, I forced my body to get moving. When I dropped to my knees to see if he was all right, he wouldn't respond or even open his eyes.

"Jack! Jack!" I said, pressing my hands to his chest and feeling for his heartbeat. I found it after a few seconds. But it was the only way I could tell that he was still alive. Later, Violet told me that Zack and Mr. Pitt ran into our house to get Dad while she called 911 on her cellphone. Somewhere in the distance, I heard Mrs. Pitt's gravelly voice offering water or a blanket or maybe it was both, but I don't remember exactly. I was so scared. I don't even know how I remembered to breathe. I just sat there holding Jack's hand and telling him *you're okay, you're okay, you're okay.* Over and over again. Like if I said it enough, it had to be true. It was probably only a minute, but it felt like hours before Dad got there.

"What happened?" he asked, crouching beside me.

"He hit his head."

Dad lowered his ear to Jack's face and listened for his breath. Then he cradled Jack's head like he was a little baby and spoke to him in a soothing voice.

"Can you hear me, Jack-Kerouac? It's Daddy. You're going to be just fine. It's time to wake up now."

I don't know if my brother heard any of it. But Dad's words definitely helped to keep *me* calm while we waited for the ambulance. It was probably only a few minutes, but it felt like forever. I wanted to cry with relief when we finally heard the wailing siren, soft at first but getting louder and louder by the second. By the time it pulled up in front of our house, Jack's eyes were flickering open. He started to say something as the ambulance guys were loading him on the stretcher. But I never found out what because after that he started to puke.

They would only let one of us ride with him. I wanted it to be me but Dad refused.

"I need you to stay here, Daisy," he said as he climbed into the back beside Jack. "I need your help. Call Mom and Grappa and let them know what happened. Ask them to pick you up and meet us at the hospital."

Now I'm sitting with Grappa, quietly panicking in the emergency waiting room. Somewhere down the hall and beyond a pair of steely white doors, Mom and Dad are with Jack, waiting to speak to the doctor.

I shift my butt in the hard wooden chair. I hate waiting rooms. They've got to be the most depressing places in the world. This one's the same as all the others — four dingy green walls covered in smudgy fingerprints and tacky artwork. I guess the art's supposed to cheer you up and make you forget where you are. Except nobody's looking at it. Nobody ever looks at the art in a waiting room because they're all too busy worrying about the sick person they've come to see. Grappa takes my hand in his. He's wearing a huge skull-shaped ring on his pinky finger. It's so ridiculously inappropriate for a hospital, for a second I almost want to laugh. But I don't, of course. I'm way too busy trying not to fall apart.

I nibble on the soft inside of my cheek as my feet tap out a nervous beat on the floor. I so badly want to ask Grappa if Jack's going to die, but I'm too chicken to hear the answer. And if I start talking now, I'm worried the words spinning around in my brain are going to come spilling out my mouth — all my guilty thoughts about how it should be me on the other side of those doors, not my brother.

Jack doesn't deserve to be in this hospital. He never deserved to be sick in the first place. Jack's never hurt anyone in his whole entire life. He's everyone's favourite. Even mine. I've never been anyone's favourite. Well, maybe Willow's, but clearly not anymore. *I* should be the sick one. It always should have been me. But there's no point saying any of this to Grappa because, as much as I love him, he won't understand. I know because last fall I made the mistake of telling him about the deal I made with the universe. How one night three years ago, I got desperate. It was back when Jack was in the middle of the treatments that seemed to be making him even sicker than the cancer. I couldn't handle seeing him so pale and thin and tired. But it went on day after day after day and it felt like it was never going to end. And so one night when I was lying in my bed worrying instead of sleeping, I offered up a swap.

My life for Jack's.

And it worked too. The year I stopped growing was the year Jack started to get better. Grappa's the only person in the world who's ever heard this story. Problem is, he didn't believe me.

"That's just a coincidence, Crazy Daisy," he said. "You being short has nothing to do with Jack. The universe doesn't make deals with little kids."

But it happened. It did. I feel it in my bones. I saved Jack's life three years ago.

So how's it possible he's getting sick again?

The waiting-room door opens and Mom's face pops around the corner. I drop Grappa's hand and jump to my feet.

"You can come see him now," she says, waving me over. "But just one at a time. And just for a couple of minutes. He needs to rest."

"Is he okay?"

She smiles and it's the best thing I've ever seen. "Come see for yourself."

I'm out of the waiting room, charging down the hall, and pushing through those white doors before anyone can catch me. Jack's lying in bed in a tiny curtained room, sipping water through a striped bendy straw. He smiles when he sees me and holds out his knuckles for a bump.

"It's a concussion," Dad says, pulling the curtain closed behind me. "But he's going to be fine."

My muscles wilt with relief. "D-does he have to stay here?"

"No, they're releasing him. But he'll need lots of rest for the next few days."

"Don't leave me hanging, Laze," Jack says. His voice sounds swishy, like he's ready to fall asleep.

I sit on the edge of his bed and bump my fist against his, really gently like he's made of tissue paper. I so badly want to grab him and hug the stuffing out of him. But I'm too scared to do anything that might hurt him more. A fist bump'll have to do.

"How're you feeling, Toe?"

"Still a bit drizzly. And my head hurts. But it looks like I'll live. For now."

And then he does that thing where he crosses his eyes and sticks out his tongue like he's dying. And I know that's his way of trying to make me laugh. And for a split second, I do laugh. But a moment later, it switches into a sob. I hang my head, shut my eyes, and let it out — because at this point, a good cry is the only thing that can help after such a horrible day. My tears drip down my nose and make a sad pattern of wet circles on the nubby white hospital blanket. I feel a hand on my shoulder. And another one stroking my hair. Someone hands me a tissue.

"Aw, Daisy," Dad says after a minute, "it's going to be okay." He's talking in that same calm voice he was using on Jack earlier.

"No, it won't."

"It will," Mom says softly. And then there's a long, awkward pause where nobody says anything. "Actually, there's something we've been meaning to tell you," she adds. "And I think maybe now's the right time."

There's something hiding behind her words. I stop crying and glance up, suddenly suspicious. All three of them are watching me closely, like I'm about to do a card trick and they'll miss it if they blink.

"If this is about Jack's appointments, I don't want to hear it!" I say, swiping the tissue across my face.

Mom looks surprised at my reaction. "But I think you do. You see, Dr. Ip's office left a message yesterday—"

"Stop!" I cover my ears with my hands and shake my head furiously. There's NO way I can handle any more bad news today. Especially not about Jack.

"Daisy—" Dad says.

"Lalalalalala."

"Come on, Rabbit," Mom says, trying to coax my hands away from my head. "Stop being so silly."

"*Paperback writer, writer, writer . . .*" I've got a whole summer's worth of Music History committed to memory. I can keep going all day.

But I never even get to finish the song because something cold and wet suddenly splashes my face. I stop singing, wipe my cheek with my palm, and look around. Jack winks at me as he raises his striped straw to his lips and prepares to spout a second mouthful of water my way. I duck just in time.

"Gross. Quit it!"

"*You* quit it," he says, lowering the straw. "Now would you listen? I want you to hear this."

How can I say no to him when he's lying in a hospital bed? I can't. "Fine." I close my eyes and prepare myself for the worst.

A hand covers mine. I know it belongs to Dad because it's big and I can feel the callouses on his palm. "I wanted to tell you earlier today, but Jack asked us to wait until Friday night. He wanted us all to be together when you heard."

Mom takes my other hand. "But since we're all together now . . ." She stops for a second because her voice is breaking up with tears. *Shootsicles,* this is going to be *so* bad. I try to brace myself for what's coming next. My stomach is clenched so tight, it feels like there's a giant fist squeezing me from the inside out.

"Jack, do you want to say it?" Mom asks.

"No, my head hurts. You do it."

"Are you sure?"

"Will somebody just please say it already?" I whisper-shout.

"I'll do it," Dad says. He takes a deep breath, and I can tell he's trying hard to be strong. "You know how it's coming up to five years since they first diagnosed Jack?"

"Yeah."

"Well, Dr. Ip and the rest of the team decided to order a complete round of tests. Five years is a pretty big deal, it seems."

I open my eyes a crack. "That's what those appointments were for?"

Dad nods.

"Okay. And?"

He smiles a wobbly smile. "And the tests came back clear. Every one of them. Jack's remission is complete. And after five years that means . . ." Dad's face suddenly crumples like he's in pain. His blue eyes flood with tears. "That means he's cured, Daisy."

I look around, trying to absorb what he's just said. Mom's crying too. And now Dad's pulling her into a hug that's so tight, I can't even tell where he ends and she begins. They sway slowly, weeping quietly in each other's arms. Meanwhile, I can't seem to move. I think my heart might have stopped.

"Cured?" I say, looking at Jack.

"Slam dunk!" he says. He smiles and pumps a weak

fist in the air, like it's the NBA championships and he's just scored the game-winning basket.

Before anybody can stop me, I hop into bed beside Jack and throw my arms around him. I'm crying one second, laughing the next. If a doctor or nurse walked in right now, they'd think I'd lost my mind.

"Hey, make room for us," I hear Mom say. A moment later, the thin mattress dips and four more arms join our huddle as Mom and Dad squeeze onto Jack's bed. There's more crying and laughing and lots more hugging. And I guess now we're officially a hippy-dippy looney-tunes sandwich.

"Why'd you take so long to tell me?" I demand. Because now I'm annoyed too. I don't like being the last one to know.

"We just found out the results yesterday," Mom says.

"Yeah, but you were all being so mysterious! I thought for sure you were hiding bad news."

Dad shakes his head. "We weren't trying to hide anything. It's just that we didn't know what the test results were going to show."

"I'm sorry, Rabbit," Mom says, dabbing her eyes with the sleeve of her shirt. "We didn't mean to make you worry." She leaves our huddle, pulls her bandana off her head, and sinks down onto the edge of a chair. Her shoulders droop as she lets out an exhausted breath. She looks like she's just finished running a marathon.

I guess, in a weird way, she has.

Suddenly, the curtain slides back with a zing. It's Grappa. He's standing there with his hands on his hips and looking none too pleased.

"There you are!" he growls. "I've been sitting in that waiting room for so long, my butt was fusing to the chair." He pauses for a second as his grey eyes sweep over each of our tear-stained faces. "Everything okay in here?"

I hop out of the bed and go to hug him, pressing my cheek against the cool leather of his motorcycle jacket.

"We're good, Grappa."

"Hallelujah!" he says. "Now let's get the heck out of here."

*

On the car ride home, Jack rests his head on my shoulder. After a few minutes, he falls asleep so hard he starts to snore. I think it's funny, considering it's not even dinnertime yet. But Mom and Dad explain how he's going to need lots of sleep and quiet over the next few days because his brain's got to heal from the concussion. They whisper this, of course, so they don't wake him up. We're about halfway home when they ask me to explain exactly what happened with the Pitts. I tell them everything I can remember: Zack's discovery of the petition, and the city council meeting to change the bylaws. I hope I get the details right, but I can't be sure.

"He said the meeting's happening tomorrow."

Mom mutters something under her breath. Can't be sure from where I'm sitting in the back seat, but it sounds like the kind of swear Grappa would approve of.

"Looks like maybe we're going to need a lawyer, Nate," she says.

"Come on, Frieda," Dad replies. "You know how much lawyers charge. Besides, how would we ever find someone on such short notice?"

"What choice do we have? Unless we—"

"Unless we what? Move to a new house?"

She shrugs as she makes the left turn onto Bond Street. Her fingers are gripping the steering wheel so hard, her knuckles are like little white rocks. "I don't know. Maybe we should just do it? Give them what they want and pull the vines down. It's a big job, but it'll probably be easier than battling it out with an appeal. Not to mention cheaper."

Dad's staring at her like she's just sprouted wings and a tail. "How can you say that? We can't give in to bullies. Ever. Think about it, today they want us to cut down our vines. If we give them that, what are they going to demand of us tomorrow?" He thumps a fist onto the dashboard. He's so upset, his beard is shaking. "I refuse to be bullied into changing our house to suit someone else. Or paying money we don't have for a lawyer."

Mom pulls in to our driveway and switches off the engine. She sighs, leans over, and rests her head on Dad's shoulder. Like all she wants to do is fall asleep.

Just like Jack.

"You're right," she says softly. "We shouldn't give in."

"You'll see. Justice shall prevail," Dad says, running a hand tenderly over her hair.

Of course, he couldn't pass up the opportunity to throw in one of his corny quotes.

I just wish I could believe him this time.

Chapter 17

Dear Willow,

I'm mad at you. I don't even know why I'm writing you this letter since you've barely written anything back all summer, but I thought you might want to know that Jack's going to be okay. He isn't getting sick again after all. Actually, Dr. Ip says he's officially cured now (!!!) except he got a concussion yesterday after we had a fight in the driveway with Violet and Zack and the evil Pitts. It's a long story, but Mr. and Mrs. Pitt have been collecting signatures from everyone on Bond Street and they want to force us to take down the vines. Later this afternoon, I'm taking the bus to city hall to fight for the Jungle and I'm so nervous, I already feel like barfing even though it's not for a few hours. I wish I didn't have to go, but the Pitts are out to get us, and it looks like my parents are leaving everything in the hands of justice, and Jack's got to rest in bed. So that leaves me.

This morning, I went online at the library and officially signed up to make a deputation, which as far as I can tell, is pretty much the same thing as a speech. I just finished writing it, but I don't know if it's any good so I woke Jack up and asked him to listen to me say it, since he's not allowed to read anything with a concussion. He said "that's very eloquent" then pulled the blanket up over his head and went back to sleep. I think he was just trying to make me feel better. I haven't told Mom and Dad that I'm going because I'm worried they'll try to stop me. And if they try, I'd probably let them because part of me's not even sure why I'm doing this in the first place because sometimes all I ever want is to see those stupid vines come down. I'm confused. And scared about seeing the Pitts again and the whole deputation thing. I wish you were coming with me. Even though I'm still mad at you. I'm not sure I'm brave enough to do this. But I think I have to try anyway.

xo

Daisy

P.S. I'm not even going to ask you to write me back this time. That's how mad I am.

P.P.S. Violet and I made our own flip-flops for Arts and Crafts last week.

P.P.P.S. Did I tell you about Zack's dimples? They're so deep, I think I they could hold a grape. Weird, right? I'm going to ask Violet if she's ever tried to stuff one in there.

P.P.P.P.S. What would you rather: Give a deputation in front of a room full of strangers? Or eat a spider sandwich?

P.P.P.P.P.S. I would choose the sandwich.

Chapter 18

I must have practised my deputation at least three times on the bus ride to city hall. Mumbling under my breath, and pointing, and stomping my foot at all the really important parts, and crossing out some words, and writing other ones in. I probably looked like one of those people nobody wants to sit next to.

I know this because, even though the bus was full, nobody sat next to me.

The meeting isn't scheduled until two o'clock but I got here extra early to make sure I didn't miss it. I've been sitting here biting my fingernails and feeling pukier with every passing minute. Now it's almost time for it to start. And yup, I'm definitely ready to barf. Right here in the heart of city hall. I glance around, scoping out my options. Do I have time to make it to a toilet? But what if they call my name while I'm there? Will I lose my turn to speak? Maybe I should just aim for the nearest trash can? *Fritz.* I should have brought a plastic bag with me.

I lean over, stick my head between my knees, and take a couple of long breaths. In, out, in, out, like I'm sipping air through a straw. After a minute, the salty taste pooling in the back of my mouth starts to fade.

You got this, Daze.

Another minute and the barf sinks back down to where it belongs.

Good barf.

I lift my head slowly, glancing around to see if anyone noticed my mini-crisis. But all eyes seem to be focused on the round bald man sitting in front of a microphone at the front of the room. He's in the middle of a long table of suit-wearing, bored-looking grown-ups. To his right, a lady with a leopard-print head scarf is typing very quickly on a computer. The clicking of her keyboard sounds like a stampede of small animals. To his left, a guy with a dreadlock ponytail is scrolling through his iPhone. Three brightly coloured flags hang lazily on poles behind the table, their edges fluttering from the breeze of the air conditioner. I wish they'd turn it up a bit. It's warm in here. I'm sitting alone way at the back of the gallery. Mr. and Mrs. Pitt are sitting together in the first row. Both of them dressed up in clothes so neat and crisp, they look like a pair of freshly made beds. They spotted me a few minutes ago. Let's just say they didn't exactly look happy to see me here.

There's a tap on my shoulder. Startled, I spin around to see Zack and Violet, hunched over and grinning at me from the row behind mine. My heart does a little happy dance. Between her flashing braces and his winking dimples, they're an awesome sight.

"What are you guys doing here?" I whisper.

"We snuck out after they left," Violet whispers back. "We knew they were on their way to city hall, so we hopped in a cab and came too."

"We want to be here to support you," Zack adds. "And maybe help if we can. How's Jack?"

"He's resting, but okay. It'll be a few days before he's feeling himself."

The room goes quiet as the bald man starts speaking again. "Next up on the agenda," he says, tilting the rim of his glasses slightly, "is a proposal to amend Bylaw 1418 — To Provide Standards for the Maintenance of Property."

"I think this is us," I say, sitting straight up in my seat. The bald man clicks his pen a couple of times and writes a quick note on his paper before continuing.

"Mr. and Mrs. Pitt, residents of 370 Bond Street, are requesting the addition of the term 'unsightly vines' to Section 6 of the municipal code, entitled 'Landscaping.'"

"*Booooo,*" I hiss under my breath.

"Each speaker will have up to five minutes to make their deputation. Our first speaker of this meeting will be Mr. Karl Pitt, representing the residents of Bond Street. Please come forward when you're ready."

Mr. Pitt stands and slowly makes his way to the front of the room. I glance over to where Mrs. Pitt is sitting alone. Her face is tight with worry and she's wringing her hands together so hard, it looks like she's kneading the world's smallest ball of dough. Maybe it's because she's not wearing that ginormous gardening hat, but she suddenly seems so small. And frail. I think back to the words I yelled at her yesterday. That stuff about her hating kids.

Why do I suddenly feel like the lowest life form on the planet?

Mr. Pitt leans in to the microphone and clears his throat.

"Ladies and gentlemen of the committee," he says, "thank you for considering our request. My wife and I have lived in our house for the past forty years. In fact, we were one of the first families to move onto Bond Street. However, in the last ten or so years, we've had to endure the overgrown monstrosity located directly beside us. And, as I'm sure you'll agree, it is just too much. Please allow me to demonstrate," he says, picking up a small remote control and pointing to a photo of my house that's suddenly flashing over a large screen at the front of the room.

"I'd like to submit these photographs as evidence of the visual nuisance we've had to endure," he continues. With a click of a button, he flips through several more photos of my house, taken from the front yard, backyard and both sides. My mouth drops open as I stare up at the big screen. The photos make the Jungle look all kinds of awesome — green, and lush, and bursting with life. Now he's scrolling through some close-ups. There's one of Jack's pet chickens, bright white against the emerald-green backdrop of the house. There's one of the baby squirrels, poking their pink noses out from the tangle of vines. There's one of the Jungle in the morning light, dewdrops sparkling on the leaves like tiny jewels. And another one of my little attic bedroom, wrapped up like a living birthday present.

It looks so beautiful. How have I never seen my house like this before? Behind me, I hear Violet gasp. I turn around to see what's wrong. She's on her feet. Her face has turned almost as red as her hair. "Those are my photos!" she says. "From my camera. Uncle Karl must have downloaded them when I wasn't looking."

"Violet, sit down," Zack hisses. "Why would he use your photos?"

"The committee probably had a rule about using professional-quality photos. So he took mine." She practically growls that last word. I glance around the room. The bald dude's staring right at us. And he doesn't look happy.

I hold a finger up to my lips. "Shhh. You're going to get us in trouble."

"I don't care!"

"Order in the gallery," the bald man says, rapping his knuckles against the table.

"Sit down, Vi," Zack says, tugging on her sleeve. "Getting yourself thrown out of here isn't going to help Daisy."

I guess that must make sense because she reluctantly slides back into her seat. I breathe a sigh of relief and turn back around. The slide show's over and Mr. Pitt's still speeching away like nothing's happened.

"I'd also like to submit this petition, signed by the other households on Bond Street," Mr. Pitt says, holding up the list of signatures. It's definitely the same one from yesterday's tug-of-war. I can see the smudgy spit circle in the middle. "As you can see," he continues, "all the residents of our street agree that these vines are unkempt and horrible to look at. We no longer want to see them every day. It is very offensive and we are in great need of your help. My wife and I would be grateful if the bylaw can be amended and the vines removed, or at the very least, cut back to our specifications. Bond Street used to be a very pleasant place to live. My neighbours, my wife and I would like it to be that way again." And with those words, Mr. Pitt salutes the committee, picks up his papers, and returns to his seat.

The bald man is busily mopping his shiny head

with a tissue. "Thank you, Mr. Pitt," he says. "Next up to speak is Mrs. Rebecca Smythe of 365 Bond Street."

I watch in surprise as Mrs. Smythe, the lady who lives in the house across the street from ours, makes her way to the front of the room. She looks all fancy in her navy-blue dress and pearls and her hair poofing out around her head like a fluffy grey cloud. She's even wearing makeup. I know this, because the large red birthmark on her left cheek is almost completely invisible. I chew on my thumbnail while I wait to hear what she's going to say. I hope it doesn't have anything to do with Bobcat and her Maltipoo.

Mrs. Smythe clears her throat and adjusts the microphone. "Ladies and gentlemen of the committee," she says, and I know she must be nervous because the hand holding her speech is shaking. "Mr. Pitt was not being truthful when he said that everyone on our street wants the Fishers' vines to come down. I'm here representing three families who don't agree and have refused to sign the petition. Unfortunately, Mr. Lee is not well enough to attend this meeting and Ms. Da Silva is unavailable. But they've asked me to speak today on their behalf. We think that the Fishers are lovely people. Frieda and Nate are hard-working parents. The children, Daisy and Jack, are polite and always willing to lend a helping hand to a neighbour in need. Yes, their vines might be growing a little bit wild, but that shouldn't be a crime. Personally, I don't think it should be anyone else's business but theirs. Thank you."

With that, she turns her gaze in my direction and smiles. Then she tucks a stray curl behind her ear and makes her way back to her seat. Violet, Zack and I burst into a round of applause.

The bald man scratches his chin and makes a couple of notes on his paper. Is that a good sign or a bad sign? I wish I could see what he's writing.

"All right," he says, clicking off his pen. "Up next to speak, we will have Mr. and Ms. Pitt of 370 Bond Street."

For a second, I'm completely confused. The Pitts are going to speak again? Then suddenly there's a scuffling sound behind me. I turn to see Violet grabbing Zack's hand and pulling him to his feet.

"That's us. Come on!" she says.

Next thing I know, she's dragging him down the

aisle toward the front of the room. A moment later she's got the mike out of its stand and she's holding it in front of her like she's a rock star and the rest of us are her audience. Her braces flash brilliantly under the fluorescent lights.

"Hi, everyone, my name's Violet Pitt." She curtsies and waves the microphone in front of her brother's face.

"I'm Zachary Pitt," he says, shoving his hands into his pockets. The tips of his ears are red as a pair of ripe apples.

"We've been living next door to the Fishers for almost four weeks," Violet continues. "And in all that time, we've never been bothered by their house. Or the vines."

"Never. Not for a second."

Down in the front row of the gallery, Mr. Pitt is standing and waving his arms. Like he's a movie director desperately trying to end a bad scene.

I cover my face with my hands so I don't have to watch.

"Violet and Zachary!" he barks. "Stop this right now!"

I peek through my fingers. The bald dude looks annoyed at the interruption. He raps the table loudly. "Order in the gallery! Please take your seat."

Mr. Pitt sits, but doesn't stop talking. "I'm sorry, but these are my great-niece and nephew! And I haven't given them permission to be here."

"Mr. Pitt, please be advised that this meeting is open to all members of the public. Nobody in this room requires your permission."

"But—"

"There will be silence during the deputations." The bald dude nods at Violet. "You may continue, Ms. Pitt."

I let out a deep breath and lower my hands. Mr. Pitt sinks back into his seat. He looks like he's chewing on a cactus. What's he going to do to them when this is all over? Is it possible to ground a kid for life?

"Thanks," Violet says. "And you should know that those were *my* photos you saw up on the screen earlier, taken from *my* camera. I took those photos because I think the vines are beautiful. And unique. And I've never seen a house like Daisy and Jack's."

"Me neither."

"My brother and I don't think something should be against the law just because it's different."

"Yeah."

"If that were the case, all of us would end up in jail for something."

"Yeah."

"Daisy's house is . . . It's . . ." Violet pauses as she searches for the right word. Zack takes the microphone from her.

"Extraordinary," he says, and his voice is like melted chocolate over my ears. "Daisy's house is extraordinary." His eyes search the room until they find mine. Now his whole face has gone full-out pomegranate. My heart skips a beat. And that's the moment I know for sure. He likes me. And somehow, I think I kind of like him too. Like, *really* like him.

How did that happen?

Violet grabs the microphone back. She points her finger at the committee table. "Do the right thing, peapods! And thanks for listening," she says, with a flourish and a bow. Then she takes Zack's arm and leads him back to the gallery. I stand and clap so hard my hands hurt. But I barely notice the pain because I'm too busy fighting back more of those stupid happy tears. Why does that keep happening?

"You guys are the best," I say, as soon they're back

in their seats. "But Ray and Karl are going to kill you for real now."

"Forget about it," Violet says, waving me off. She's grinning like she's just won the lottery. "After yesterday, we're already in trouble. The worst they can do now is send us home. And there's only a couple of weeks left of summer anyway."

I glance over at Zack. I want to thank him, but I'm suddenly too shy. So I duck my eyes and turn around to see who's speaking next. The bald dude is shuffling through a stack of papers like he's about to start dealing a hand of crazy eights.

"Moving right along," he finally says, straightening his pile of papers with a sharp *clack, clack* on the table. "We will have Ms. Daisy Fisher up to give her deputation. Ms. Fisher is representing, um . . ." He squints and adjusts his glasses. ". . . Jungleland."

Chapter 19

My heart is thumping so fast, I think it might explode.

Rubbing my sweaty palms on my jeans, I grab my notebook and walk slowly over to the little table at the front of the room. Oh *nerds,* how I wish Jack was here instead of me! This would be so easy for him. He'd be his charming, loveable self and have this whole committee eating out of the palm of his hand in no time. I take a second to adjust my chair, flip to my speech, and take a deep breath.

"Hello," I try to say, but no sound comes out. I swallow and try again. My throat feels like someone's squeezing it with a fist. I wish I remembered to bring my puffer with me.

"Hi," I manage to say a bit louder this time. "My name's Daisy Fisher and I'm twelve years old. I'm here to tell you why you should please leave my house alone."

"Speak up please," says the leopard-print-scarf lady. Her fingers hover over her keyboard, ready to pounce.

I swallow harder, trying to clear the lump that's clogging my throat.

"When I turned eight, I made a wish on my birthday cake. I wished the vines growing over my home would come down so I could be just like other kids. More than anything in the world, I just wanted to be normal. That was a long time ago. I'm twelve now and a lot smarter. And I'm here to say that I've changed my mind about that wish."

I glance up from my notebook to make sure the committee's still listening. They're all watching me closely. The guy with the dreadlocks has put his phone down. The bald dude's taking notes. And leopard-scarf-lady's fingers are flying. I lick my lips and turn the page.

"I mean, what does normal mean anyway? It's just a made-up idea that some people use to attack others who aren't like them. I think 'normal' means something different to everybody. For me, normal is my home — weeds, vines and all. And normal means having parents who respect nature, instead of fighting with it. And normal means putting family first, before anything else.

That's what my mom and dad taught me. That's what they did when my brother, Jack, got cancer."

My voice is breaking a bit now and I have to bite my lip and wait a second until I feel okay to continue.

I will not cry in the middle of city hall. I will NOT cry in the middle of city hall.

"Ms. Fisher, do you need to take a break?"

I shake my head. If I stop now, I'll never be able to finish.

"I'm okay," I say, forcing out a wobbly smile. One, two, three deep breaths.

"I realize that Mr. Pitt and some of our other neighbours have a different version of 'normal' than my family. But why should their version be more important than ours? Do we really need a bylaw that says one house should look like all the others on the street? There's no law that says I have to wear the same clothes as my neighbours, is there? Because — sorry, no offence — Mrs. Pitt wears a hat I wouldn't want to be caught dead in."

Someone in the room giggles at that, which makes me giggle too. I steal a glance over at Mrs. Pitt but she won't meet my eyes. And suddenly I wish I could take the hat comment back.

"Ms. Fisher," the bald dude says gently, "your five minutes are almost up."

Already? I nod and hurry to find my place on the page.

"Also, Ms. Fisher, please refrain from including disparaging remarks in your deputation."

"I know. Sorry." My cheeks go warm. I dip my chin so nobody will see. Peeking through my curtain of hair, I glance around the room. I feel so small sitting here in front of all these adults. The committee members are all watching me silently, waiting for me to finish. And suddenly I'm closing my notebook and putting it aside because I think I know what I've been trying to say all along. And it's not written down anywhere except inside my head.

I point to the back row where Violet and Zack are sitting. "I have a friend who believes pictures can tell a story better than words. I hope the pictures she took of my house made you see how beautiful it really is. Mr. and Mrs. Pitt might not see it that way. But they shouldn't be able to tell me to get a haircut if I don't want one. Or force my dad to trim his beard, even if it really is way too shaggy. So why should they have the power to decide what our house looks like?

We're the only ones who get to decide that. I'm not a lawyer, or a professor. I'm not wise or college educated. I'm just a kid. I have two parents, a brother, a cat and a home where I've lived my entire life. And believe me, none of us are what most people would consider to be 'normal.' I'm glad that dumb birthday wish never came true, because somewhere along the way, I've figured out that I don't really want to be the same as everyone else. Why would anybody want that? Would you rather live a phony life trying to be like someone else in the world? Or live a happy life being true to yourself?"

I pause for a moment and take a shaky breath.

"One of my dad's favourite quotes is 'beauty is in the eye of the beholder.' My family might not be great gardeners and my house might not be neat and tidy, but they're beautiful to me and I wouldn't trade them for anything. Please don't change the bylaws. The vines aren't hurting anybody. Thank you very much."

There's a whoop and a burst of applause from the back of the room. Out of the corner of my eye, I see Violet and Zack jumping up and down and cheering. Grabbing my notebook, I stand and make my way back to my seat.

Violet grabs me up into a squeezy bear hug.

"That was incredible!" she squeals into my hair, so loud my right ear starts to throb.

"You were great!" Zack says. He's grinning so wide his whole face looks like one big dimple. He's holding his hands awkwardly behind his back, like they suddenly weigh a ton and he doesn't know what else to do with them.

"Thanks," I reply, feeling my cheeks go pink again.

"Will everyone please be seated?" the bald man asks with an exhausted sigh. It's obvious he means the three of us, so we sit our butts down fast. "Thank you. This will be the final deputation before we vote," he continues. "Our last speaker will be Mr. Nathan Fisher, resident and co-owner of the property in question, 372 Bond Street."

I freeze in my seat. *Did he just say what I think he said?*

He did.

Holy.

Stromboli.

I don't know where he came from, but there's Dad sitting in the seat I just left. He's wearing his security-guard uniform and looking very officially important. I think he's even combed his beard.

"Thank you for the opportunity to register my objection to the Pitts' petition," he says, pulling the microphone up to meet his height. "I appreciate you hearing me out on such short notice. I have a deputation prepared; however, I won't be delivering it today after all. After hearing my very wise daughter speak, I've decided I don't have anything of further value to add." He swivels around in his chair, looks right at me, and smiles. "She said it perfectly."

And with that, Dad gets up and takes a seat not far from the Pitts in the front row of the gallery. I want to run over and hug him but I don't know if that's allowed and I really don't want to get in trouble with the committee. I think the meeting's almost over and the last thing I want to do is jinx it. The bald man makes another note on his paper and tucks his pen behind his ear.

"Thank you for those impassioned speeches," he says, glancing at his watch. He covers his microphone with his hand and turns to say a few words to the lady next to him. For a few seconds, the room is silent except for the low hum of the air conditioner. Are we all done? I sit straight up in my seat, ready for the vote. He uncovers the microphone and nods his head.

"The Property Standards Committee will now take a short recess to consider the matter before we put it to a vote."

Recess? Awesome. Immediately, the committee members at the front of the room start turning in their seats and talking amongst themselves. I make my way up to where Dad's sitting.

"Hey."

Somewhere under his beard, I think I see a hint of a smile. "Hey."

"Soooo," I say, peeking up at him from under my eyelashes. "Am I in trouble?"

"For what?"

"Well, you know . . . This." I wave my hands around the gallery. "Sneaking out and coming here to make a speech."

Dad strokes the straggly ends of his beard. "Well, no, I don't like it when you sneak around. But considering I'm here at city hall, I can hardly be upset with you for doing the same." He drops his hand and shrugs. "Besides, I knew you'd be here."

My jaw falls open. "How?"

"I couldn't sleep today. Guess I was too nervous about the meeting. Just before lunch, I went to check on Jack. He told me everything. To be honest, though, I was planning on coming anyway."

I can't believe what I'm hearing. "You were?"

"Well, sure. I couldn't let this go without a fight."

"But what about that thing you said to Mom, about justice always prevailing?"

He scratches the back of his head. I think there might be a smile building behind his beard, but it's too hard to tell for sure. "Yeah, well . . . You know what they say: Sometimes justice needs a helping hand."

Should have known a corny Dad-quote was coming. "Let me guess," I say, rolling my eyes. "The Dalai Lama?"

"Nope." He's full-out grinning now. And that little spark in his eyes is shining brighter than I've ever seen it. "Nathan Fisher."

He opens his arms and I scoot into them for a hug. "Just to clarify," he adds, "did you really tell city hall that my beard is too shaggy?"

"Yup."

"Frieda put you up to that, didn't she?"

"Just remember: beauty, beholder and all that stuff." I give his furry cheek a quick kiss before pulling away. "I have to go take care of something. Be right back."

I take a deep breath. Before I lose the last drop of courage I have left, I walk over to where the Pitts are sitting.

"Hi," I say.

They stare at me blankly. You'd think I was a Martian who just landed on their lawn and announced my plans to take over the planet. For a second or two, I'm not sure they even heard me. Finally, Mrs. Pitt's pencilled eyebrows float up in surprise. "Hello," she replies, watching me warily.

"I . . . I wanted to let you know that Jack's going to be okay. It's just a concussion."

Mr. Pitt's steely eyes soften a bit. "We know," he says with a nod. "We called the hospital last night to check but they told us he'd already been discharged."

They called?

"Okay, great." I chew on my thumbnail and stare down at my shoes. "I also wanted to say that . . . I'm sorry for being rude earlier. And for saying you hate kids."

Mrs. Pitt's mouth tightens. She glances over at her husband. "Well," she finally says, "I suppose we're sorry then too. For acting as if we did."

I let out the breath I didn't know I'd been holding. "I also wanted to ask you not to be mad at Violet and Zack. They were just being good friends and fighting for something they love. I hope they won't get in trouble for that."

I really hope that last part wasn't pushing my luck. Before either of the Pitts has a chance to reply, the bald man starts speaking again.

"This meeting is called back to order," he announces into the microphone. "Everyone please take your seats."

There's a lot of chair scuffling and feet shuffling. I dart back to the empty seat next to Dad. I peek at the Pitts as I plop into my chair. Their wrinkled hands are clasped together like they're praying. After about a minute, the bald dude holds up his hands for silence.

"Committee members will now vote by a show of hands," he says. "All in favour of the motion to amend Bylaw 1418?"

This is it. The pukey feeling in my stomach suddenly

comes roaring back to life. The Pitts lean forward in their seats. I hold my breath and watch as four of the committee members raise their hands.

"All against?"

One, two, three, four, five hands rise up.

Four to five! *We won!*

"The motion does not pass," the bald man announces. He lowers his notepad and looks right at the Pitts. "The proposal to recommend an amendment to Bylaw 1418 is hereby denied."

I jump to my feet and do a victory dance in front of my chair. Somewhere behind me, I can hear whooping and cheering and I know it's coming from Violet and Zack. In front of me, the Pitts are shaking their heads as they gather up their stuff.

Bald dude waits for the room to settle down before continuing. "However," he says, "I would like to add that, after reviewing Mr. Pitt's evidence, we do have a recommendation." He pauses for a second to check his notes while I drop my bum back into my seat. A recommendation? I have a sinking feeling about this. It's never good when someone starts a sentence with "however."

"For health and safety reasons, the residents of

372 Bond Street are encouraged to keep their windows and doors clear of vines and overgrowth." He peers at me over the top of his glasses and points at me with his pen. "Fresh air and sunshine will help you grow big and strong, young lady."

I think my cheeks might actually be melting.

"Yes, sir," I whisper.

Because what else can I possibly say to that? Guess I should just be grateful he didn't call me "Weed."

*

The car ride home is quiet. It's been a long day and the last thing I had to eat was a piece of sugarless gum on the bus ride to city hall. But I don't even know if that counts as something to eat, because you don't swallow gum so technically it's not like real food. Right? So yeah, I'm way too tired and hungry to talk. I wonder if this is what a runner feels like after finishing a marathon. Except less sweaty.

Dad gets it. He lets me chillax while he battles the rush-hour traffic back to Bond Street. I keep my window rolled down so I can feel the breeze on my face while I try to imagine what Mom's going to say when we tell her about the committee's recommendation to clear the vines from our windows. Will she want to do it? She didn't exactly look thrilled when she saw what Grappa and I did to Jack's room. And then I start thinking about Violet and Zack. I wonder what their punishment is going to be. Are the Pitts going to send them home? Am I ever going to see them again?

By the time we pull up in front of the Jungle, it's dinnertime and the heat from the afternoon sun's starting to fade. Mom's polka-dot scooter is parked in the shadow of the garage, which means she's home. I sit up and click off my seat belt, excited to tell her about our big win at city hall today. Tilting my head, I gaze out the window at the evening sky. The cloud bellies are streaked pink, like the world's ready to celebrate.

Dad shifts the car into park. "You did great today, Daisy. Really great." He smiles and the skin around his eyes crinkles like potato chips. "Your speech was beautiful — full of passion, honesty and wisdom. You're going to make a most-excellent writer someday."

"Thanks, Nate," I say, tracing a happy face in the dashboard dust. "You did great too."

"Aw, I didn't really do much of anything," he says. His smile and the potato-chip crinkles fade a bit.

"Yeah, you did," I say, adding three more happy faces to my doodle. "You were there. That was everything."

I blow the dust fuzz off my fingertip and push open the door to get out. That's when I notice the engine's still running. I glance over my shoulder. "Aren't you coming?"

"Sorry, honey, but I have to get to work. My shift's going to start soon." He yawns and waves me on with a flick of his hand. "Go ahead inside. Frieda should be there. She took the afternoon off to stay home with Jack."

I get out and wait at the edge of the driveway, watching as the car pulls away. Dad gives the horn two little toots, like he's saying "bye-bye" in car talk. I wait until he disappears around the corner of Bond Street, enjoying the fresh evening air on my skin. The days are starting to get shorter. Which means Willow will be home from camp soon. Normally, I'd be counting down the hours. But this year, I don't know what to think.

My stomach growls. I turn and hurry up the driveway, dying to grab a bite to eat and see how Jack's feeling. I want to tell him about everything that happened this afternoon at city hall with the Pitts and Dad and Violet and Zack. But when I go to let myself in, the front door's locked. I'm about to ring the bell when I pause with my finger in mid-air.

What if Jack's still sleeping? I don't want to wake him up.

Swinging around, I head through the gate to the backyard. But when I turn the corner around the snowball bush, I freeze in mid-stride. There's Mom, sitting in the middle of a giant pile of leaves. Her eyes are closed and her legs are crossed like she's in a yoga pose. Our ladder's leaning against the house. I glance up. There's a big chunk of vines missing from one of the windows.

"Frieda? You okay?"

She opens her eyes and smiles. Maybe it's the fading daylight, but her forehead looks as smooth as glass.

"How'd it go, Rabbit?"

"Uh, great," I say, wondering where to even begin to explain what went down today. I decide to lead with the best part. "We won."

"Oh, wonderful!" I wait for her to ask for more details, but she doesn't. Instead, she pushes some leaves together to make a little cushion and motions for me to come sit beside her. "I'm glad you're home," she says. "I need your help."

Chapter 20

So the vines are coming down. Well, some of them anyway.

While Jack slept his concussion away this afternoon, Mom said she sat in the backyard and did some thinking — about our house and our family and about Jack being cured and how this was like a new beginning for all of us. And she thought about how happy Jack was after Grappa and I cleared his window. That's when she decided more of the vines had to go.

"Enough is enough," she tells me, curling an arm around my shoulder. "It's time for a fresh start."

"You want to pull them *all* down?"

She shakes her head. "No, no. Just over the windows."

"But won't they grow back? You said that's what happened the last time. Remember?"

"Well, when that happens, we'll just climb back up and pull them down again."

I'm about to tell her how that's exactly what the bald dude on city council told us to do. But in the end, I decide not to say anything. If I know Frieda, she wouldn't want to think it was anybody else's idea but her own.

Nibbling on my thumbnail, I stare at the newly naked window above our heads. Bobcat's perched on the ledge, staring down at us, his black tail flicking the air behind him.

"It's going to look so different," I say, picking up a handful of leaves from the ground beside me and spreading them across my legs.

Mom tightens her arm and pulls me closer. I turn my face into the soft skin on her neck. The smell of her coconut cream fills my nose.

"Yeah. But I think it'll be for the best. For Jack . . . For all of us."

"Okay," I say. Pushing the leaves off my lap, I jump to my feet. "Then let's do it."

We work at the windows for another hour after dinner, and then again for a couple of hours the next day. But it's too big a job for the two of us to handle alone, so we save the rest for the weekend when the whole family can pitch in.

Grappa comes over Saturday morning and Jack's feeling better and we put out a pitcher of homemade lemonade and a bag of kale chips and tune the radio to our favourite station. At first, Dad was calling it our "vine-killing spree" but Jack didn't like the sound of that so we ended up changing the name to something less violent. Now it's our "clearing-the-windows party," which isn't as catchy but we're all going along with it to make Jack happy. Today, the goal is to finish the back of the house. We only have one ladder so we all take turns. Right now it's my turn to sit in the shade and bark out directions. I'm happy about it, because that's what camp directors do best.

It doesn't take long before Grappa's joining me in the shade.

"Someone should be here to keep you company," he says, helping himself to a second glass of lemonade. Personally, I think he's just worried about getting his fancy leather shirt sweaty, but I don't say anything. Right now Jack's running around trying to find new homes for the refugee birds and bugs and rodents that are getting displaced. And that's okay because Hurricane Frieda doesn't look like she needs much help up on that ladder. She's got her green bandana, her gardening gloves, an assistant (Dad) and a new pair of shears. And she's going after those vines like clearing them's an Olympic event and she's determined to win gold.

Little by little, all the windows at the back of the Jungle start opening up and it's like watching a giant leafy advent calendar come to life. *Sif, sif, sif* go the vines as they fall in a heap to the grass below. I'm watching the tangle of vines coming down and the naked windows emerging, and I know this is going to sound weird, but it's like I'm seeing a baby being born. It's kind of exciting, because I know a change is on the way. But it's emotional at the same time. And also a bit sad.

Like a sunset.

Or the end of summer.

Grappa finishes the last of the lemonade and asks for more, so I go to the kitchen to make some. While I'm there, the phone rings. I drop what I'm doing and rush into the living room to answer it. Maybe it'll be Violet or Zack. We haven't seen either of them in four days — not since the big showdown at city hall. Which I guess means the Pitts decided to ground them after all. I miss them a lot. So does Jack. He told me that one night last week he saw some lights flashing in his window and I wonder if it was Violet trying to send us a message in Morse code. I told him I've been thinking about going over there and ringing the doorbell, but he convinced me not to because what would I do if one of the Pitts answered?

I'm not sure what the answer to that is.

Earlier this morning, I thought I saw a pair of binoculars pointed at me from one of the Pitts' upstairs windows. I waved, just in case it was Violet. Or Zack. But it was probably just my overactive imagination.

I answer the phone on the third ring. "Hello?" I say, breathlessly.

"Daisy?"

I'm so shocked when I hear the voice, I almost drop the phone.

It's not Violet.

Or Zack.

"Willow?" I gasp.

"Yeah, hi. How are you?"

Her voice sounds stiff and polite. Almost like she's talking to a stranger.

"I-I'm fine," I stammer. There're suddenly so many

questions swirling through my head, I can barely think straight. *What's wrong with you? Where are my letters? Are we even still friends?* An awkward pause roars through the phone line. "Is camp over already?" I ask instead. My voice sounds stiff too. This sure doesn't feel like a conversation with my BFF.

She clears her throat. "Almost. I came home a couple of days early. I . . . I got your letter about city hall. And how mad you were at me. I was worried."

I don't even know what to say to that.

"Aren't you going to talk?" she asks.

My feet start pacing nervous circles around the room. I'm clutching the phone so tightly, I might never let go. "I don't know. What do you want me to say?"

"You still sound mad."

"I am."

"Daisy—"

But I don't let her finish because all the worry that's been piling up these past few weeks comes pouring out of me in a flood of angry words.

"Two *shizzling* postcards!" I yell. "You never wrote me one letter! Not one! And all of a sudden you're worried about me? Why are you even calling? Do you even want to be my friend anymore?"

“Of course I do,” she says quickly.

I’m pacing so fast now, I’m starting to sweat. “Really? You could have fooled me.”

“Please, Daisy . . . Just stop. I . . . I have something to tell you,” she says, and I know by the sound of her voice that whatever it is, it’s going to be big. A lump of nerves rises in my throat. I stop pacing.

“Oh, *crux*. Are your parents divorcing too?”

“No. That’s not it.” I can hear her sucking on her bottom lip. She always does that when she’s nervous. “I didn’t write you letters because I kind of have, like . . . a boyfriend.”

I switch the phone to my other ear, just in case this one’s not working right. “A whatdidyousay?”

“A boyfriend. Braden and I met at camp last summer. He’s nice and super funny and we were only ever just friends. But then he started texting me this spring and at first it was just once in a while, but then it was every day, and all of a sudden we weren’t just friends. It was more. And I was so afraid to tell you. Because, well, you know . . . we had a pact never to have boyfriends. But I felt horrible because every time I tried to write you a letter and not mention Braden, it felt like a giant lie. I thought postcards would be better because they're shorter, but each one I sent just made it worse. And it got to the point where I knew I couldn't write another word until I told you the truth. But I wanted to do it in person, not in a letter." She stops talking to take a breath. "I'm really, really sorry."

My knees feel wobbly, like I'm standing on octopus legs. I sink down onto the couch. "You were *afraid*? That's why you didn't write?"

"Do you forgive me?"

"But . . . You're never afraid. Of anything."

She laughs, but it's more sarcastic than LOL. "Everyone's afraid of *something*, dooberdog," she says.

My head plops back into the cushions. A boyfriend? This isn't at all what I was expecting. I need a couple of seconds to sort through my thoughts.

"Dude! Say something!"

"What do you want me to say?"

"Say you forgive me!" she says, and I can tell by her voice that she's making her pitiful-cute face. "Pleeeeeease?"

Do I forgive her? I guess so. I mean, of course I do. How can I stay mad at Willow? Especially when she puppy-begs. Before I know it, all my anger's melting away.

"Yeah, we're good," I say. And I mean it.

She breathes a sigh of relief. "We can still build our house together, right? I mean, if one of us ever has a boyfriend, he could just stay in the garage. Or the guest cottage."

"Okay, but uh . . . we don't have a guest cottage in the plans."

"So, let's put one in. Can I come over?"

"Now?"

"Yeah."

I jump to my feet and go peek out the door to the backyard. Mom and Dad are still working away at the vines. Grappa looks like he's fallen asleep in the shade. Jack's climbing the chestnut tree. "Okay. How fast can you get here?"

She giggles in my ear. "How about now? Go open your door."

Say what? I dash to the front and pull it open. There's Willow, all suntanned and smiles and holding up her cellphone. She clicks it off when she sees me and throws her arms around my neck. I hug her back and we squeal and jump up and down and, for a minute, I'm sure I'm never going to let go.

She asks if we can go to my room to get the file with

our house plans. I say yes. Of course. Then, on our way up the stairs, I ask the question that's been burning into my brain for the past ten minutes.

"So, this Braden dude . . . did you kiss him?" I ask, turning to watch her answer.

She giggles. "Once. But it wasn't gross like it looks in movies. It was actually pretty okay."

Don't know why, but I'm sort of relieved to hear that.

We climb the last few stairs and push open the door to the attic, but I freeze before I even take a step inside. Willow's right beside me. When she sees my room, she covers her face and screams into her hands.

My mouth opens, but nothing comes out. My window's been cleared. The afternoon sunlight spilling through the glass makes my whole room look like it's been drenched in honey. It's like how heaven must look — bright, and warm, and so beautiful all I can do is stand there and stare.

"Where'd your vines go?" Willow demands.

"Gone," I say, walking over to the window. And, oh my God, I can see out! I peer into the backyard. Mom's still up on the ladder, pulling down the last of the vines from over the bathroom window. I tap on the glass. She looks over and waves a handful of leaves at me.

"Come on. Let's go see how it looks from outside."

We tumble back down the stairs and out the door to the backyard. When I see my house from this angle, I'm so stunned, I can barely speak. Mom's finishing up with the vines at the top, while Dad's on the ground raking the leaves into piles.

Dad spots us and comes over. "Doesn't it look great?" he asks, wiping his sweaty forehead with the back of his hand. "Your mom's right. I think we're all ready for some change around here."

I take a few steps back so I can see the whole thing. It does look good. Beautiful, actually. And sort of ridiculous too — kind of like that time Dad went to work with his pants accidently tucked into his socks.

I glance over at Willow. She looks like she's going into shock. And then I remember about the birds.

I grab Dad's arm. "What about the nest outside my window?"

"Don't worry. Jack's already found a new home for it." He leans over and points to the chestnut tree. "Right over there. See?"

I follow the line of his finger until I see it. There it

is, tucked between two sturdy branches. And not all that far away from my attic window.

"Better get back to work," Dad says. "We're going to start on the side windows now. Tomorrow, we'll tackle the front. Are you two going to help?"

"Yeah, sure," I say, standing on my toes and craning my neck to kiss his furry cheek. Mom and Dad look happy about this, which makes me happy too. But I think Mom's right. It's going to take a bit of time to get used to. I love my new sunny room, but when I look at all those vines lying in a tangled heap on the ground, there's a tiny ache in my chest. And I feel like I do when I think about growing up.

I wonder how it's possible to be homesick when you're standing in your own backyard.

Chapter 21

These days it feels like everything's stuck on change. First Willow and her boyfriend, then the windows' de-vination. And now Dad. In honour of the Jungle's new look, he decided to shave off his beard. The whole thing. He didn't even leave a small patch to remember. And he didn't tell any of us he was doing it until it was done. Maybe he was worried we'd try to stop him.

Maybe we would have.

I was upset at first. His face reminded me of a freshly peeled potato. Jack was upset too. We both thought it was like having a stranger walking around with Dad's corny quotes and voice. But as shocking as it was, we got used to it pretty fast. By the time he left for work that night, I was already feeling better. The little gold spark was right there in his eyes, so I knew deep down he was still the same Dad.

Mom said she likes this freshly peeled version of him much better. No more scratches on her cheeks.

School starts next week. Yesterday, when I went to try on some of my fall clothes, I was shocked to find they fit small. Half my jeans were too tight and all my long-sleeves were too short. Mom was really excited when I told her. She made me try everything on again so she could see for herself. She said I must have had a growth spurt.

Huh.

Looks like I'm changing too.

Then she hugged me and smiled and I saw some of those happy-sad tears in her eyes, just like I get sometimes. And that got me thinking . . . maybe I inherited more from Mom than just her weird toes.

Right before dinner, I overheard her telling Dad about my growth spurt. She said it must be because of all the fresh air and sunshine I'm getting now that the windows are clear. But I think I know the real reason I'm growing again. Jack's finally cured. So the deal's all done.

Willow's promised to take me shopping for new clothes this weekend. She's been coming over every day since she got back from Couchikoo, which means Junglecamp's officially back in session.

The only thing missing is Violet and Zack. Summer's coming to an end and I honestly didn't know if I was ever going to see them again.

Then earlier today, the doorbell rang in the middle of Arts and Crafts. I ran downstairs to answer it before the noise could wake up Dad and, *holy stromboli*, there they were standing on the front porch. All glittering braces and flashing dimples. I was so happy to see them, I almost fell over.

"Where have you been? Have you guys been grounded all this time?"

"Nope," Violet said. "After what happened at city hall, Aunt Ray and Uncle Karl took us up to their cottage on Fairy Lake. They said they wanted to spend some 'quality time' with us before we had to go home."

"Really? Quality time?" I asked. "How'd that go?"

She glanced at her brother and shrugged. "Actually, it was kind of fun."

Then Zack explained how they were leaving to go back home to their parents, but their aunt and uncle gave them permission to come say goodbye. "They aren't really so angry at you guys anymore," he said. "Especially now that you took some of the vines down."

Violet groaned at the mention of the vines. Like it hurt just thinking about them. Then she gave me a scrapbook of all the photos she took of the Jungle before the window-clearing party. We bear-hugged and promised to write letters. She told me her favourite quote from *Charlotte's Web*: "It's not often that someone comes along who is a true friend and a good writer."

For a second, I thought I was going to cry.

"Maybe you can come stay with us next summer," Violet said. "I'm sure our parents will have worked their divorce out by then. We have a cottage on a lake back home too. It's almost like a real camp."

"That would be great," I said. I wanted to ask if I could still be the director. But I didn't. Guess it's only fair to let someone else have a turn.

When it was time to say goodbye to Zack, I suddenly got shy.

"Bye, Daisy" he said. Pushing his baseball cap back, he leaned down and kissed my cheek. Lightning fast. And it wasn't horrible. Like, at all. His lips were as soft as a pair of feathers. When he pulled away, I could see his face had gone pomegranate again.

"If I write to you, will you write back?" he asked.

I felt my face go warm too. "Yeah."

That made him smile and I so badly wanted to reach out and trace a finger around one of those dimples. I didn't, though.

Maybe I'll save that for next summer.

I felt his kiss on my cheek for hours. All through dinner, and after my shower, and into the night. When I see Willow tomorrow, I think I might have to tell her to add a second guest cottage to the plans.

I miss the vines outside my window sometimes, but mostly at night. There's nothing to shush me to sleep now, and the air is so quiet it hurts my ears. Every now and then, I hear the neighbourhood dogs barking at each other and I wonder if they're plotting their next move in the battle with Bobcat. But even though the vines over my window are gone, I can sometimes still hear the house talking to me. Like tonight. It sounds like one little word whispered over and over again: *Wee-eeed, wee-eeed, wee-eeed.*

And it makes me smile. Because suddenly that nickname's not all kinds of wrong anymore.

I stare at the stars twinkling in my window and think about everything that happened this summer. How I figured out that normal's not all it's cracked up to be. And how things aren't always going to stay the same, no matter how much I might want them to. And how that's okay. And how sometimes life's not all that different from a crossword puzzle. How there's usually a solution lurking behind the blank spaces. You just have to keep trying different things to find the one that fits.

I flip my pillow to the cool side and wait for sleep to come. And just when my brain is almost done shutting down, I know what I want to write about for my book. And it's so obvious, I start laughing into my pillow.

What took me so long to figure it out?

Switching on my flashlight, I pull out my notebook and turn to a fresh page.

Acknowledgements

This little book you hold in your hands has taken several years and a collective effort of galactic proportions to bring into the world. I'd like to thank these bright, shiny people for helping me along the way.

Thanks to my intrepid crew of first readers — Helaine Becker, Hélène Boudreau, Francine Gerstein, Mahtab Narsimhan, Gordon Pape, Kim Pape-Green, Suri Rosen, Simone Spiegel and Frieda Wishinsky — for cheering me through the first few drafts and on to the finish line.

Heartfelt thanks to April Young (aka Director of Fun) and late, great Jerry Doren (aka King of Yorkville) for delivering so much spirit, style and creative inspiration over the years.

Thank you to the Ontario Arts Council for generously supporting this project through the Writers' Works in Progress and Writers' Reserve programs.

Many thanks to Sarah Heller for her ongoing guidance and support.

Huge thanks to the wonderful team at Scholastic, most especially Diane Kerner, Erin Haggett, Aldo Fierro (for the brilliant cover design) and the incredible Anne Shone for her encouragement, wisdom, humour . . . and for saying "yes."

Hugs to Jonah and Dahlia for their enthusiasm, love and unflagging honesty.

And finally, a universe of gratitude to Jordy — for everything, for always.

About the Author

Deborah Kerbel is the author of eight books for children, young adult and middle grade readers. She lives and writes in Thornhill, Ontario, with her husband, their two book-loving children and a schnoodle named Alfredo.

Her novels have been shortlisted for the Canadian Library Association's YA Book of the Year Award, the Manitoba Young Readers' Choice Award and the Governor General's Literary Award. She is the recipient of the City of Vaughan's RAVE Award recognizing her work as a Mentor and Educator in the Literary Arts.